BAKER'S DOZEN

Soul Mutts | Book One

LORI R. TAYLOR

STERLING & STONE

Chapter One

BAKER SCOOTED CLOSER to the wall at the back of her cage, pressing against the wire mesh until she felt the cool cement wall through her fur. Her favorite place to sleep, not just because it made her cage seem bigger, but because it put her out of reach.

The air smelled strange, like the rough hands that scrubbed and pinched and poked her. All those people scents mixed with the sharp smell of urine, the dry savory of kibble, and the scent of fear or happiness from the other dogs.

This wasn't her first time in a place like this. But she didn't want to spend too much time thinking about that. Her legs got shaky when she did, and her chest felt empty, like her heart had dropped into her belly.

Somewhere in the building, a door slammed. Baker lifted her head, looking down the row of cages filled with fellow unlucky dogs, but she couldn't quite see to the end.

Didn't matter.

The terrier with spotty ears in the cage opposite hers sat upright and alert, brown nose pressed against the gate, gnawing the metal every now and again.

He wanted one of the humans to come and take him away.

Baker didn't. She knew better.

"Right through here," said a voice, before a flurry of barks broke out.

The spotty-eared terrier barked and hopped on all fours, wagging his tail.

"It all depends on what kind of temperament you're looking for." It was the soft-spoken, darker-skinned woman who ran the place. Leslie, the other humans called her. Leslie didn't try to touch her when she didn't want to be touched, and she didn't make her go out into the yard to play, either.

Not like her last owner. Michael had pretended he was nice, but then he kicked her, and hit her, and—

"I'm looking for an animal who will be a companion." The reply was from another woman, who smelled like flowers.

The last time Baker had seen flowers, Michael had jerked her leash so hard she'd choked, and dragged her behind him to the car, then brought her here.

"—prefer it if it was a female dog. One with a more docile personality." The voices were closer now, and Baker dropped her head, lying as still as she could.

Spotty Ears hopped up and slammed his paws against the fencing.

The two women stopped in front of Baker's door.

She glanced up at them, without raising her head. She'd learned in the past few days that the more bored she looked, the less interested the humans would be in her.

The dark lady wore a long coat with a pattern on the front pocket and stains all over: muddy paw prints and a splash of food. The other woman, the one who smelled like flowers, bent down and peered at Baker.

"That's Baker." The dark lady smiled. "She's a boxer mix. Very shy."

"Oh." The flowery woman had long gray hair, and her

hands clasped a big black bag in front of her. She reached inside it and brought out a smaller flat black box — Baker had seen some of the other humans use these things before. They had lights and pictures on them, and sometimes made strange noises. "Do you mind if I take a picture?"

"She's probably not the dog you're looking for," Leslie said, sounding uncertain but unwilling to argue with the other person.

"My husband loves boxers. And my son, Michael—"

A low growl built in Baker's throat, and her lips slid back over her teeth at the sound of that name.

The flowery woman took a step back, her smile flattening.

"I'm sorry, she's been through a tough time," Leslie said. "She's not quite ready for—"

"She looks dangerous. You should get rid of her."

Humans. They only pretended to be nice.

Leslie straightened, and her shoulders stiffened. Her voice was just as stiff. "We don't 'get rid' of dogs just because they've had a rough go of it."

"She's clearly aggressive. Who's going to want a dog who growls and—?"

Baker let out a yapping bark, the fur on her back bristling.

"I think you'd better leave." Leslie stepped back and gestured for the woman to walk down the long corridor. Once they were gone, the other dogs settled down.

Spotty Ears across the aisle stayed a moment longer, sniffing and licking the fence. Finally, he huffed and retreated to the other side of his cage. He sat on his blanket and placed his snout on his paws, eyebrows lifting as he looked around, though not at Baker.

None of these dogs liked her. Fine. She didn't like them either.

But she couldn't leave with a human like that. Not after Michael, not after the girl who kept forgetting to come home and feed her, and not after the old man who had left her in the park.

She closed her eyes and tried to sleep.

~

"SO, WHAT HAVE WE GOT TODAY?"

Baker's eyes snapped open. She recognized the voice — Dr. Dale. He poked Spotty-Ears with a needle, twice, while another human held him so he couldn't get away.

She stayed at the back of my cage, hoping he wouldn't notice her.

He wore a long white coat, and he stood next to Leslie holding a flat piece of wood with paper on it. He tapped a thin black pen against the sheet.

"We still haven't gotten any shot records for Bruiser," Leslie said. "Eliza's called twice, but no one is answering."

"Hmm." Dr. Dale clicked the pen against the clipboard. Then he clicked it again. "If we don't get anything by tomorrow, we'll just assume he's had nothing and start the series. Bruiser the Chihuahua, ha. Someone had a sense of humor."

"Wait until you meet him," Leslie replied.

Dr. Dale laughed once. It was warm, full sound. Baker started to wag her tail. Then she forced it to be still. She didn't want them to think she cared they were there. At least Dr. Dale didn't want to take any dogs away, and neither did Leslie. So she just needed to stay out of reach whenever he returned.

"I see Baker's still here."

"She isn't causing any trouble," Leslie said. "I think she's getting better."

Dr. Dale made his lips thin enough to disappear.

"Les, no one's doubting whether your heart's in the right place, but if you don't send some of these dogs to other shelters ... there's not going to be a shelter left here to keep them in." Dr. Dale touched Leslie's shoulder.

She took a step back and shook her head, but she didn't show her teeth or snarl at him. "Pretty Paws will always be here."

Baker stayed as still and small as possible, but the fear in Leslie's voice scared her. This shelter was at least better than the last one, where they'd made her go outside, and a bulldog had bit her, and the man who had given her food sometimes skipped days.

"Baker's spot could've gone to an adoptable dog. Maybe several, she's been her so long."

"You don't understand, doc." Leslie crouched in front of my cage. "She's different."

"How?"

"She needs help."

"They all need help."

"Not like her." Leslie sighed. "Look, she came from another shelter, and her previous owner was abusive. She deserves a second chance as much as any of these other dogs do."

Her brown eyes were so warm, Baker's tail kept wanting to wag, even though she told it not to.

"Downright inspirational," Dr. Dale said, chuckling. "Just … if we want to keep this place running, we're going to have to make some changes. Or bring in a lot more donations."

Leslie sighed, placed her hands on her knees, and pushed herself upright. "Baker's not ready to go yet, but we'll get her there."

"If some of them don't go soon, they'll all have to go."

Leslie lifted her palms. "You've done enough grilling for the day, doc. You must have been a chef in another life."

Dr. Dale chuckled, clicking the pen again. "Lord knows, you weren't a comedian."

Another door slammed.

Baker flinched. She couldn't get any closer to the wall of her cage, but she tried anyway.

Spotty Ears jumped up again and barked, accompanied by a chorus of whining and yipping from the others.

"Excuse me, but this is an employees only—" Leslie stopped, mid-turn. "Jeremy." The word sounded rough. Like a bark gone wrong. "I'd say it was good to see you again, but—"

"Yeah, yeah, I know, you'd be lying." Jeremy waddled into view. He wore a blue shirt and dark pants. He had a thick, black stick strapped to his side and a hat on his head. "Sorry to do this to you, Leslie, but I've got another complaint."

"Not again."

"Yeah, again. Leo from the pizzeria next door." Jeremy tucked his fingers into his belt as he chewed something minty-smelling with his mouth open. "Again."

"That's ridiculous." Leslie put her hand on her hip. "We're a shelter. Of course the dogs are going to bark occasionally."

"He says it's chasing away his customers." Jeremy chewed for a moment. "He's a crotchety old you-know-what, but ain't nothing I can do about this. I don't follow up on the complaint, it's my neck on the line."

She nodded, but her lips had gone droopy at the corners. "Let's talk about this out front. I need a breather, anyway."

Once the humans were gone, everyone settled back down. Except Spotty Ears, who kept turning in circles and nibbling at his tail.

Baker didn't want to leave this shelter, but if she stayed here too long, they would put her in another one. A worse one.

That meant the next old lady who came in would have to take her home.

No matter what.

Chapter Two

"I'm sorry, ma'am, but that's not going to be possible."

No, no, no. This was not okay. Maeve had finally found the courage to take a leap of faith — and she'd leapt face-first into a brick wall.

Except that the wall was a private banker named Greg, who looked at her like she was a bug on the underside of his shoe. If the bug was also coated in dog poop.

"Please," Maeve said, keenly aware of how saying "please" would probably make this worse. Guys like Greg loved it when people like her begged. "Look, I'm a total whiz in the kitchen. You should try my éclairs. In fact, if you give me, what like … a couple hours, I could come back here with an éclair to sweeten the deal?"

"There is no deal, Miss Watts. You simply don't qualify for a loan this big. I can't, responsibly, take the risk on you when you're an unknown, and your credit score—"

"That's not my fault."

"—isn't exactly what it should be."

"That was my ex," Maeve said, hating that she'd even had to bring him up. "He used my card. I — look, can you just give me a break? This is my dream. Haven't you ever had a dream, Greg?"

He looked at her like she'd asked him if he'd ever picked his nose. Apparently Greg wasn't a dreamer.

Or maybe he dreamed about spreadsheets and credit scores and business plans. How could she say that in business-speak?

Maeve had no idea. So she tried talking to him like a person. "I've been stuck in a really terrible job for a long time. I'm a freelance graphic designer. You have no idea what that's like."

Greg stayed silent, the blue light from his PC screen illuminating his *whatever, lady* expression.

"People never know what they want, Greg. Know what I'm saying? Whether it's the color or the design or the brightness or the size or … but I do. I know what I want, and it's to open a bakery."

"Miss Watts—"

"It's all I've wanted, for the longest time. But I never took the leap. I always found an excuse." She clasped her hands in front of her chest, like she was praying to St. Greg, Patron of Unbirthed Dreams and Personal Loans. "The past six months showed me that it's time to finally take the leap. You can understand that, right? That this is a big step for me?"

"I can't give you the loan, I'm sorry. Not without collateral."

"Did I mention I have a car? You could take my car, if I don't pay you back. Which I won't." *Oh, shoot.* "I mean, I will pay you back. So you won't need to take my car."

"Even your house wouldn't be enough collateral to cover the requested amount," Greg said. "But you weren't willing to offer it anyway. If you don't believe in your dream enough to put everything you've got behind it, why would we?"

Maeve flushed. He had her there. Mom had left it to her — the only place that had ever felt like home — and she couldn't bear the thought of some other family baking cookies in the kitchen where Mom had first let her crack the eggs and read the Tollhouse recipe off the bag of chocolate chips.

Some other family eating lasagna in the dining room that Mom had painted aqua and decorated with seashells and sand dollars when she was pregnant with her. They used to pretend to be mermaids in there, until Maeve got old enough to start feeling silly playing pretend.

Some other family watching TV in the living room, where they'd watched old movies together after Mom's chemo treatments. Her appetite had been gone then, and when she took a nibble of Maeve's latest brownie experiment, it had only been to humor her.

No, that house was hers, and it was going to stay hers.

Greg rose from behind his perfectly-organized desk and walked to the door, which he opened and held for her. "Good day, Miss Watts."

Maeve stifled a groan and stood, searching for a new argument as she made her walk of shame toward the door.

She paused just outside the office, turned to face him. "If you could find it in your heart to take a chance on me, I'll prove to you that—"

Greg's office door slammed shut.

"Great," she muttered. "That's just great."

Now what? Greg had been her last chance — none of the banks in town would give her a loan, saying the same thing Greg had. It didn't matter that her jerk of an ex had ruined her credit, or that she was working crazy hours to pay off the debts he'd racked up in her name.

It didn't matter that everyone who'd ever tried her cookies said they were the best they'd ever eaten.

It didn't matter that she was tired of designing website graphics for clients who either micromanaged her or expected her to read their minds.

Maeve strode through the bank, head high like Greg the

Dream Killer had just offered to loan her a million bucks, because nobody else needed to know that this was her walk of shame. She didn't let her shoulders slump until she was outside, where the morning sunshine was watery and the air was ridiculously chilly.

Welcome to spring in Logan's Creek, the smallest town in southern Ohio.

She drew her cardigan closer to her chest, then took a breath. The banks wouldn't help her? Fine. She'd just have to come up with the money for the bakery on her own.

Or … maybe Greg the Dream Killer was right. What did Maeve know about starting a business? She didn't have the experience, a plan, she didn't have a penny. She didn't have a hope.

Chin up, girl, you've got this.

She walked down the street, passing wrought-iron lamps, quaint benches, and glass-fronted stores on the way to her car — which was scratched up, old, and definitely not worth any kind of collateral. But it ran, didn't it?

Everyone was always so worried about how things looked, but just because something looked bad on paper doesn't mean it didn't *work.*

Her phone buzzed in her tote as she opened the car door and got inside.

She dumped the tote on the passenger seat and fumbled the still-vibrating phone out.

Her stomach sank.

It was Leroy, her least favorite client. And unfortunately, the one who sent her the most work.

So Maeve unlocked her phone and went to the message app.

I've decided I like green. But a different shade of green. The one you used in the logo was too faded. I need something more vibrant.

"What, like puke green?" she asked out loud, her fist closing around the phone, squeezing until the plastic creaked.

She could ignore him and reply later. Pretend she'd lent her phone to her mom to play *Silly Lizards*, so she hadn't seen his text right away.

Three dots appeared.

Are you there? I'm on a tight schedule. We need to talk ASAP.

Every inch of her wanted to throw the phone across the car. But Maeve couldn't afford to replace it — or the car's windshield — until Leroy paid her for finding him a shade of green that met his exacting standards.

Instead, she locked the device, stuck it in her bag and took a breath. Leroy's graphic design emergency could wait an hour. Or three.

This morning would've been a lot more productive if she'd spent it baking.

She drove home, humming a tune under her breath to cheer herself up, and failing miserably. After all, home was empty. And even though she definitely didn't want to get back together with David, the quiet that fell over the house when it was just her felt … weird.

She parked in front and made her way to the front gate, which opened onto a quaint stepping-stone path up to the front steps and the wraparound porch.

Mom's house, the only thing Maeve had left of her. The fact that she'd ever invited David to stay with her was just plain annoying. Now all her fond childhood nostalgia was tainted by memories of all the fighting they'd done before the breakup.

Once inside, she threw herself onto the living room sofa and buried her face in the pillow. A scream built in her belly, then stuck at the back of her throat.

She almost wished she hadn't tried — at least then, she could have the fantasy of her own bakery to keeping her going when the world's Leroys made her want to quit.

But now, knowing her dream was doomed and that she

had nothing but Leroys to look forward to? Leroys for the rest of her life?

No.

Maeve refused to let the Leroys win.

She sat up, grabbed her laptop off of the coffee table, and fired it up.

There it was. The stupid design she'd done for Leroy.

"Go away," she muttered, minimizing the program.

Her LiveLyfe profile popped up, with a live feed to display what everyone was doing. Including David.

Ugh. She wanted to block him, but it felt kind of petty to do it now.

Maeve had never been able to open up to anyone. Then she'd met David, and he taught her it was okay to be vulnerable. That crying wasn't a big deal. That allowing love into her life was the best possible thing for her.

What a joke. Apparently, he was being vulnerable with a gorgeous blonde right now, on a boat off the coast of Hawaii.

His feed showed everything Maeve didn't want to see, including David's new girlfriend's perfectly-sculpted abs and bleached hair.

Not that she wanted him back. Good luck to the model. Good luck to them both.

She slapped the laptop lid shut and rubbed her forehead — she'd been frowning so hard, she was en route to a headache.

Enough.

She couldn't let the Davids win, either. But what was she supposed to do instead?

She needed to bake something.

Since she'd been dumb enough to add David to all her credit cards, she was trapped in freelance graphic design hell — all the money she earned from the Leroys went toward paying those off. But her living expenses were covered by the money she made teaching baking at the community college, for their culinary arts program.

She could go in and prep for tomorrow, maybe whip up some cranberry-orange oatmeal cookies to take to the hospice where Mom had spent her last few days.

Leroy could wait.

MAEVE SIGHED, smiling at the neatly printed recipes she'd stacked for tomorrow, and the prepared ingredients, all separated in their containers. Her class was for beginners, but they'd worked their way up to baking muffins, and she was excited to share one of her secret recipes with them.

A basic carrot-cake-style muffin, studded with pecans, sweetened with applesauce, and spiced with cinnamon, plus a hint of cardamom.

Okay, so not exactly the most exciting — they weren't double-chocolate truffle muffins — but it would be a step up from the oatmeal raisin cookies they'd made last week. Or tried to, in some cases.

Poor Freddie (her favorite student) didn't have the gift, but Maeve gave him an A+ for always trying so hard.

The timer on her phone dinged. She pulled two sheets of cookies out of the oven, her mouth watering in anticipation. This had been Mom's favorite recipe. And despite the fact that the community college's kitchen wasn't exactly Michelin-star quality, the ovens held an even temperature, which is why the browning around the cookies' edges where the butter and sugar had caramelized was perfect.

It was so easy to close her eyes and imagine herself standing in her own little bakery, with a room full of hungry customers demanding more Crème Puff Supremes or donuts with maple syrup glazing.

"Knock, knock."

Maeve's eyes snapped open, and she blushed at being caught daydreaming. She checked that her hairnet was in place as she smiled at the director of the college.

Nate was in his early fifties, but gray from having three middle-school-aged kids who couldn't sit still in class. He gave her a grin and came over to the counter, nodding at the cookies she had yet to put on the cooling racks. "Those smell amazing. May I?"

"Give them a minute, or you'll burn your fingers." Maeve grabbed the spatula and started transferring the cookies to the racks.

While he waited, Nate picked up one of the recipes from the pile and scanned it. "I think I'll stop by after tomorrow's class and see if I can convince one of your students to part with a muffin or two."

"In good conscience, I have to warn you not to try Freddie's. But you could come by and make your own."

"Oh no, I'm a terrible baker." Nate put down the recipe. "But this is exactly why I came to see you. I've just heard that the campus is hosting a healthy baking competition. Sponsored by the HealthNut Corp. Heard of them?"

"They do those vegan snacks, right?"

"They're offering a huge cash prize for any contestant who can come up with a delicious sweet treat for their new product line." Nate grabbed a cookie from the rack, took a bite, and grinned. "You deserve a little reward for your talent."

"Talent, sheesh," Maeve said, blushing. "I just like to bake."

"Freddie just likes to bake. You're an artist."

She wrapped three more cookies in a napkin and handed them to Nate. "For the little ones."

"Seriously, enter that contest and do us all proud," he said on his way to the exit. "I'll be back tomorrow to steal some muffins."

"You gotta bake 'em if you wanna eat 'em," she called after him.

While the cookies cooled the rest of the way, Maeve loaded the dirty dishes into the dishwasher and got it started. She didn't want to get her hopes up, but the contest made her stomach feel fluttery just thinking about it.

And hopeful was such a nice change, after the total poop fest this morning had been.

If she won the contest, she could use that money to fund her bakery. The massive exposure wouldn't hurt either — being associated with the HealthNut Corp would be big for anyone starting a new business.

Her nerves swelled. She shifted her weight from one foot to the other.

You can do this.

If she was brave — or stupid — enough to march into a bank and beg for a loan without collateral, Maeve sure as sheep's wool was brave enough to enter that competition.

HER STOMACH CRAMPED with anxiety all the way down the hall to the administration offices. But the closer she got, the more weight her feet seemed to gain. A competition like this would be advertised heavily, and that meant she'd have serious competition. What if she didn't make it? What if her treats weren't good enough?

David's cheating had been humiliating. Having to grovel to clients like Leroy was humiliating in a different way. It was getting harder and harder for her not to feel like a total loser.

How much harder would it be if she lost this contest, too? And with it, her last chance to start her bakery?

Mom used to say that no one can make a person feel inferior without their consent. Maeve thought Eleanor Roosevelt had come up with that, but she'd heard it from Mom first, so she always thought of her when she heard it.

She set her jaw. She'd just have to make something good enough to win, because no way would she let this opportunity pass her by. This was literally her last chance at doing what she wanted to do.

The door was open, but Maeve knocked before entering anyway.

Mrs. Lieberman, the elderly receptionist, shifted her horn-rimmed glasses and looked past the other woman in the office. "Hello there, Maeve. Come for information about the HealthNut competition?"

Everyone at the college was familiar with Maeve and her aspirations, possibly because she hung out in the cafeteria boring them all with her dreams. Plus, she'd helped Mrs. Lieberman find her cat the other day.

The other woman in the office, a brunette whose long, wavy locks fell well past her tan shoulders to a blue paisley sundress, turned toward her. "Well, if it isn't Maeve Watts."

The cramping in Maeve's stomach got more intense.

There were only three things that could dampen her spirits.

One: David. Because he was an idiot.

Two: the fact that she couldn't get a loan.

And three: Jassie St. Clair, her high school nemesis.

"What are you doing here?" Maeve asked, even though she already knew. Jassie was all about country clubs and horse riding, but they shared exactly one interest.

Baking.

In school, her pastimes had included pulling Maeve's skirt up in front of the most popular guys in the school, shadowing her during Home Economics, and spreading vicious rumors behind Maeve's back. The most colorful had been about the time their teacher had gotten sick — Jassie had told everyone she'd poisoned her with a bad cookie.

Maeve's pastime had been avoiding Jassie whenever possible.

"Cat got your tongue?" Jassie's gaze wandered from her face down to her battered high-tops, taking in the old jeans and Mom's favorite T-shirt on the way.

Maeve wished she'd changed at home, but how was she supposed to know she'd run into her nemesis here?

Jassie looked perfect, as usual. Seriously, shrink the woman and put her on a doll stand. Did people do that? Did they keep dolls on doll stands?

"I'm just surprised to see you here. It's been a long time." It was a lame excuse, but whatever. She didn't have to explain herself to Jassie.

"Did I hear correctly?"

"What?"

Jassie twirled a strand of glossy hair — she had to be using shellac to get that kind of shine — around her finger. "That you're entering the baking competition. For HealthNut?"

"You sound surprised."

"I guess I forgot that you were still working at the community college. Part-time, right? Or did they finally offer you a full-time position?"

Maeve crossed her arms. "What's your point?"

"I just figured you would have accepted that it takes a lot of talent to make it as a pastry chef and moved on by now. Unless you've got a baking show I'm not aware of?"

That was the worst thing about Jassie, right there at the bottom of a very long list. She never just insulted you outright; she always merged onto the most passive-aggressive route.

"Not all of us happen to be spoiled trust fund babies," Maeve said, because she had no trouble insulting anyone who rubbed her the wrong way. "Some of us have to earn what we get."

Jassie pursed her lips like Maeve had just given her a handful of rotten leaves and mulch.

"Good luck," she said as she snatched a sheet of paper off Mrs. Lieberman's desk. As she walked past, she whispered, "You're going to need it."

Jassie wasn't a better baker. But she was great at putting Maeve in the worst possible mood.

"Don't pay any attention to her," Mrs. Lieberman handed Maeve a piece of paper with a lot of fine print on it. "Everything you need to know about the competition. Give Jassie what-for."

"Thanks, Mrs. Lieberman." She'd give Jassie something, all right. A kick in the pants.

Metaphorically speaking, of course.

Chapter Three

MAEVE SET the HealthNut brochure on her kitchen counter.

The contest rules were simple.

She had to bake a batch of something healthy to qualify and bring it in to get taste-tested by a HealthNut judge. The deadline was in a few days.

She needed to come up with something that tasted like heaven on a plate, but that also fell within their fat-sugar-protein ratio and was under the caloric limit. And they preferred that it contain at least one superfood.

No problem, right?

She was going to keep it simple. Who doesn't love peanut butter cookies? She started with all-natural organic peanut butter, coconut nectar instead of sugar, and flour made from a mix of brown rice, quinoa, and amaranth, so they'd be gluten-free. She even substituted flax seed for the eggs, and a combination of avocado oil and walnut oil for the butter, so the cookies would be completely vegan.

These would be the healthiest cookies in existence.

But ... how would she know if they were the most *delicious* healthy cookies in existence?

Maeve wasn't just biased, she was also in completely new

territory — she was used to baking normal, buttery-sugary cookies. Did she want to win the competition so badly that she might delude herself into thinking her first attempt at a vegan cookie was delicious?

She needed an outside opinion, just like an artist needed input. Or a writer. Or … whatever. She just needed to know if her cookies were good or not.

"Sheesh, relax," she told herself. "The cookies aren't even out of the oven yet."

The timer rang. Maeve tugged on her oven mitts, then brought the cookies out and set them to rest on her granite countertop.

They smelled pretty good. Not like her normal peanut butter cookies, but these were tons healthier, so they wouldn't be *exactly* the same.

Maeve glared at them, eyes narrowed.

"You're going to be great, right?" She was tempted to grab one and try it, but she'd learned her lesson after the first (or fifth) time she'd burned the roof of her mouth to be patient and let the cookies cool first.

She headed into the bedroom, took a quick shower, and changed into a pair of yoga pants and a long shirt. By the time she got back to the kitchen, the cookies were cool.

"Here we go," she whispered, and took a bite. Semi-sweet, peanut-buttery goodness spread over her tongue. But beneath the nutty sweetness, Maeve could also taste a faint bitterness that could've been the flax meal or one of the ancient gluten-free grains. Or maybe it was because the coconut nectar had caramelized faster than normal sugar, and the cookie's bottom had browned faster than she'd expected.

The texture was different too — still dense and moist, but also a bit chalky.

She took another bite.

Pretty good. She was starting to get used to all the differences.

But maybe that was a bad thing. Would the judge take the time to get used to those differences?

Or would they expect the cookies to taste just like normal ones?

She'd try the next batch with whole-grain, stone-ground flour — her usual go-to when she wanted her cookies to lean toward the healthy side. But then her entry wouldn't be gluten-free, and that was important when it came to health food these days.

She needed a second opinion.

She put some of the cookies into a Tupperware, closed them up, and headed for the door. Her best friend, Emma, would tell her the truth. Once she had some honest feedback, she could start tweaking the recipe.

Em was an angel, volunteering at the local dog shelter on her off-days — and today was one of those days — so Maeve drove to Pretty Paws.

Ten minutes later, she pulled into the parking lot where the shelter was located, in a strip mall anchored by a Staples. Pretty Paws was tucked in between a pizzeria and a Chinese restaurant. She side-eyed the cookies where they sat fastened into the passenger seat. "Don't do anything I wouldn't do," she said, and set them free. Well, almost. They were still in their Tupperware, plotting her downfall. Or her success.

Emma would decide.

Maeve grabbed the cookies and headed into Pretty Paws. The reception area was quaint, with pamphlets about the shelter itself, how to volunteer, and why you should spay or neuter your pet.

It was as comfy as it could be on a budget, but places like this always made her a little sad. The fact that these dogs had been left behind was upsetting. Not that she was going to do anything about that — she wasn't going to get a dog herself, *ever*.

Once bitten, twice shy, right? Except for her, it was once bitten, and she'd never go near another dog again, period.

One of the volunteers emerged from a door at the back of the reception area, a young woman with bright pink hair and a name tag that read *Bobbie*. She was in her teens, or maybe just out of high school, and her smile was wide with excitement for life.

"Ma'am? Are you here looking to adopt?"

"What? No way. I mean, no thank you." Maeve tried for a laugh, but it sounded awkward. "I'm looking for Emma. Emma Tran? Is she around?"

"Oh sure, they're giving the dogs their baths. Can I call her out front for you?"

"That would be great, thank you."

Maeve walked over to the collection of mismatched upholstered chairs and sat with the container in her lap. A happy Labrador looked up at her from the cover of a magazine. She averted her eyes, choosing to focus on the cookies instead.

"Hey girl!" Emma appeared in the hallway, wearing the baggy clothes that were her uniform when she was volunteering here. She'd dried her hands, but her shirt was wet with splotches of soap and water. "I'd hug you, but I'll end up doing damage. Did you bring me cookies?"

"Kind of," Maeve said.

Emma, who'd been her best friend since middle school, took the chair next to her and brushed the dark hair back from her face. "Good. Because I am so in the mood for cookies."

"I'm assuming you've already washed the dog off your fingers?"

"Don't be toxic," Emma said, and stuck out her tongue.

"I'm struggling not to be, after the day I had."

"What happened?"

Maeve glanced over at Bobbie, who'd returned to the reception desk, but the girl seemed more focused on her

phone than anything else. So Maeve broke down her day —
the bank, Leroy and David, the competition.

"So that's what the cookies are for?" Emma asked.

"Yeah, but there's more to it than that. Guess who I saw at
the college office?"

"I'm guessing it wasn't someone nice, like Santa Claus. Or
Chris Hemsworth."

"You're still on a Chris Hemsworth kick?"

"The man plays a literal god, Maeve. Everyone should be
on a Chris Hemsworth kick."

"Well, unfortunately, it wasn't Chris Hemsworth. Or
Santa. Let's face it, there's equal chance of them being in the
community college office in Logan's Creek. It was *her*."

"Jassie," Emma said through gritted teeth. The way her
name deserved to be said. "Don't tell me she's entering this
competition too."

"You know, that thing she does?"

Emma drew herself up straight and pressed her palm to
her chest. "Oh, it's so lovely to see you again. That's such a
gorgeous bracelet — I didn't know Goodwill gave those
away."

"Exactly. But swap out the bracelet for baking, and oh, I
don't know, my future."

"Such a diva." Emma rolled her eyes. "Remember the
time she pulled up your skirt in front of—"

"Don't. The scars told me that story this morning."

"Maybe because every time Tom Fowler sees you he calls
you 'Grandma Panties.'" Emma giggled, pressing her hand
over her mouth. She cleared her throat. "Sorry, that wasn't
very supportive of me."

"To be fair, that's what I was wearing."

Emma put a skinny arm around Maeve's shoulder and
drew her into a side-hug, keeping the wet spots of her shirt
away from her. "Don't let her get to you. She's just jealous."

"Jealous? Of me?" Maeve shook her head. "Everyone's

jealous of Jassie, not the other way around. She's got a hot boyfriend, she's rich and beautiful, she can have anything she wants, and—"

"She doesn't have your natural talent for baking. A fat bank account and a country club membership don't make her a great pastry chef, as much as she wants them to."

Maeve leaned her head against Emma's for a minute, smiling. She always knew the right thing to say or do. She'd been the one cutting the gum out of Maeve's hair in the sixth grade — another of Jassie's cheap tricks.

"Now," Emma said, "how about you let me try one of these cookies before I die of starvation? Or desperation. I swear, I can smell them through the Tupperware."

"Can I have one too?" the receptionist asked.

"Sure! I need to know exactly what you think." Maeve lifted the lid, and the aroma of cookies drifted out of the Tupperware. She gave one to Emma, then brought the container to Bobbie.

Before she could snag a cookie, a shout rang out from the back of the shelter. Followed by a splash of water, a yelp, and the skitter-scratch of paws on the floor.

"What's going—?"

"Hey!" a woman yelled.

A dog slipped into the hallway and darted toward the reception area, dripping wet, its brown fur slick against its lean, muscular body.

Maeve squealed and jumped back.

But it was already too late. The dog saw her and pounced.

Chapter Four

BAKER HAD NEVER SMELLED anything so good.

It reminded her of the time when she'd snuck a bite of bread from Michael's plate that had been covered in something gooey that stuck to the roof of her mouth.

This was like that, only better, because it was also sweet.

It was coming from the container in the new lady's hands.

Baker jumped for it, slamming into the woman's belly, jaws just missing the edge of the container that held the really amazing smell.

The lady screamed and threw her hands up. The container turned end over end in the air, spilling out brown disks onto the floor. They fell and cracked into pieces.

Baker spun around them, drool dripping from her lips as she slurped up the nearest piece.

The first bite was heaven, way better than kibble. Baker licked up the crumbs greedily, then lunged for the next piece.

"Get it away from me." The lady pressed her back to the wall, next to a door that smelled like outside. Fresh air. And cheese.

This was so much better than getting a bath from the man who'd dragged her out of her kennel. Baker didn't know his name, and didn't want to learn it. He reminded her too much of Michael.

"Maeve, relax." Emma, the one with soft hands and lots of whispers, walked toward the new lady. "It's okay. She's not going to hurt you. Look, see? She just wanted some cookies."

"Oh, no. No way did she want some cookies. You saw the way she jumped at me. She wanted to bite me. She wanted to—"

"Maeve, relax, honey."

But Maeve's eyes were wide, and she was breathing hard.

Baker ate the last cookie and turned toward Maeve, tail lowered. She crouched down, water still dripping from her fur, and laid her head on her paws. Would Maeve hurt her, too?

"I know what dogs are like. I've been bitten before!"

"I know, honey." Emma petted her friend on the arm. "But look, she's not growling or anything."

"She ate the cookies. All of them. Em, those were my competition entry cookies. I needed you to tell me what was wrong with them so I could refine the recipe."

Maeve's voice was squeaky. Baker twitched.

"Look, there's still this one." The volunteer girl behind the desk lifted half a cookie from behind the counter. "She didn't get it."

Both of the other women stared at the girl as she put the cookie on the counter.

Baker wagged her tail, slowly, hoping she'd drop it by acci-dent. Those cookies were the best thing she'd ever eaten.

Maeve was still against the wall, looking at Baker like she wanted to bite her. But why would she be afraid?

Maybe a bad man had hit her too, or fed her bad things, or left her behind in the park.

Baker wagged her tail once. To let Maeve know that she understood.

"She likes you," Emma said.

"No, she doesn't," Maeve replied. "She just liked the cookies."

Baker wagged her tail again. Maeve smelled like cookies and grass and fresh air.

"Baker's shy too," Emma said.

Maeve made a hiccuppy kind of sound. "The dog's name is *Baker?*"

"According to the person who brought her in. Apparently he found her in the dumpster behind the grocery store where he worked, eating a loaf of Graceful Baker bread that was beginning to go moldy." Emma cocked her head like she'd just seen something she'd never seen before. "Pretty funny, when you think it about it. The first person Baker's ever wagged her tail at is also a baker."

"The first person?"

"She doesn't like people."

"I can relate to that." Maeve laughed. Her shoulders relaxed, and she came away from the wall. Baker stayed where she was, stilling even her tail.

"She did just give your cookies a stamp of approval." Emma walked to the counter and brought a lead from behind it. She slipped the loop around Baker's neck. "See? She's not going to bite you."

She wasn't going to bite Maeve. Baker didn't hurt people. People hurt her.

"Why don't you try petting her?" Emma asked. "I've never seen her so docile."

"She's probably just full," Maeve said.

"No, I'm serious. This is really weird. Baker's been here a while, and she's never let anyone touch her. She doesn't even like it when Leslie goes near her, and all the dogs love Leslie."

"Feed her this," the other girl said, holding up the half-eaten cookie.

Baker thumped her tail against the floor a couple of times. If she got a cookie for it, she'd let Maeve pet her all day.

"You've got to be crazy," Maeve said. "I'm not putting my hand near those teeth."

"Come on, grow a pair of ovaries. She's just a dog."

Maeve took a deep breath. Then she accepted the half-cookie from the girl and brought it toward her. Baker stayed on the floor, paws pressed flat, but lifted her head.

She didn't want to scare Maeve. She might not give her the cookie.

Maeve held the cookie on her palm, but her face was white as a sheet.

"Here, girl, this is for you."

The cookie came closer. Baker carefully ate it off Maeve's palm, licking her skin for crumbs afterward. Her other hand came down on Baker's head, and she stroked the fur between her ears.

It was nice. A warm, happy feeling bloomed across her body and legs. When it got to her tail, she couldn't help wagging it faster.

"See? She likes you," Emma said.

Maeve backed away fast. "There. I did it. Happy now?"

"You know, I'd be even happier if you actually adopted a dog."

"What? That's crazy."

Could Maeve have any more cookies? Maybe in one of her pockets?

"A dog is always better than a boyfriend, and you need company. I know how lonely you've been in that big old house of yours."

"Yeah, let's say *that* louder. I don't think everyone in Staples heard you."

The sound of Emma's laugh rolled through the room. A sweet sound, but Baker didn't wag her tail this time.

She wasn't sure if she wanted to go home with Maeve. What if she hit her for eating the cookies instead of petting her?

Baker sighed.

"Dogs are awesome," Emma said, lifting a finger. "They're loyal. They're always happy to see you. They'll never cheat on your or hurt you. They're funny. They'll protect you and your house. They'll love you unconditionally. And let's face it, we both know you're not going to be dating anytime soon."

"I'm not going to be getting a dog anytime soon, either. Especially not that dog," Maeve said. "You saw the way she jumped at me."

"She was probably freaked from being washed, dude. Besides, you were the one who threw the cookies all over the place. You're both a little jumpy."

"Thanks, I appreciate you comparing me to a dog," Maeve replied with a laugh.

"She's never done anything like this before." Emma tugged at the leash and walked Baker back toward the kennels. "You must be special."

"Or she just likes cookies," Maeve called. "Speaking of which. I have to go make another batch."

The front door slammed a moment later, and she was gone.

Of course she was.

Baker couldn't trust anyone, not even Maeve and her yummy cookies.

Chapter Five

Maeve paced the kitchen, a towel slung over her arm and butterflies making a mosh pit in her belly. Her fourth attempt to invent the perfect healthy peanut butter cookie was almost ready to come out of the oven. This batch had small quantities of almond and coconut flour, in addition to the ancient grains she'd started with yesterday. She was trying to solve the texture problem — the perfect cookie wouldn't be the slightest bit chalky.

Two days to the deadline. Not enough time to refine the recipe through trial and error.

And at this point, Maeve no longer trusted her tongue to tell her whether each round was getting better or worse.

But maybe this would be the perfect batch.

Unless she'd already made the perfect batch, and that deranged dog had eaten them all.

"Stupid dog," she muttered, and tried to ignore her guilt for having said it out loud.

But how could Emma even suggest that she adopt a dog, knowing how she'd been bitten as a child? Let alone Baker, who'd practically attacked her to get a cookie?

Besides, dogs were a lot of work. You had to feed them

and bathe them and take them for walks and who knows what else. Maeve barely had enough time for David when they were together, and he was a grown man who could feed and bathe and entertain himself.

If she couldn't handle living with a boyfriend, she definitely couldn't handle bringing a dog into her life.

Her phone dinged for the billionth time. She'd stopped checking her texts around dinnertime yesterday, because she wasn't going to reply to the thirty-odd messages Leroy had sent about shades of green, and graphic design emergencies, and was she going to reply or was he going to have to talk to her supervisor?

If she won the HealthNut contest, Maeve would never have to talk to Leroy again.

But the ticking on the oven's timer was driving her to distraction. She checked it again. Two minutes before the cookies came out of the oven, then they'd need to cool on the rack for at least another fifteen before she could taste them. The judge would be eating them cold, so she needed them to be near room temperature to get a good flavor profile.

Ideally, Emma would taste them and tell her what she needed to change, but she had another shift at Pretty Paws today, and no way was Maeve going back there so some other dog could ruin this batch.

Besides, it could take another dozen tries to get the recipe just right, adjusting it each time based on the previous batch. If Maeve had to run out of the house to get feedback on every batch, she'd never make the deadline.

She'd just have to make it work.

She tucked the kitchen towel into the front pocket of her *Don't Kiss the Cook* apron, then retrieved her laptop from the living room and set it on the kitchen counter, next to the cooling rack half-filled with the last batch of too-sweet cookies.

The timer hadn't shifted at all, still two minutes left. Had time actually stopped?

Two days. Only two days. Her heart thudded in her chest.

Maeve opened her laptop and found her LiveLyfe profile still open. Thankfully, the images of David were gone.

They'd been replaced by something even worse.

An update from Jassie St. Clair, shared by one of Maeve's supposed friends. She definitely wasn't friends with Jassie — the point had been to ignore Jassie for the rest of her natural, and unnatural, life.

No such luck this time.

Look who's finished her submission for the HealthNut Corp Baking Competition. First prize, here I come. It's all healthy, gluten-free, made with almond meal, fresh cocoa and coconut milk. Not that you need to know all the ingredients in my secret recipe!

That was the caption. Totally Jassie's style. Underneath it was the picture of what she'd made.

"You've got to be kidding me," Maeve hissed.

Jassie had whipped up a full-on, two-tiered dark chocolate cake.

So much for keeping it simple.

Worse, it was the exact same type of cake they'd made back in Home Ec. The last time Maeve had actually botched a baking project. Jassie's had turned out perfectly, impressing Mrs. Rasmussen.

It wasn't a coincidence — it was a message, aimed laser-tight in Maeve's direction. *Remember this other time I beat you?*

"Now she's being passive-aggressive through baking?" Maeve pinched the bridge of her nose, hoping against hope to ward off a headache. "Typical."

This was the challenge, the glove thrown, and she was supposed to rise to it. Should she try to outdo Jassie by making something fancier for her first entry?

Or was it smarter to keep it simple and aim for the best possible version of that simple item?

Maeve leaned in and studied the picture. Jassie had decorated her cake with faux flowers. Or real ones. Who knew? Maybe she'd decided to go so healthy and natural that she'd added in fresh grass from her front garden for extra fiber.

She struggled not to slam the laptop closed again. If she wasn't careful, she'd end up breaking it for real, and then what would she do?

Instead, she strode to the cupboards, flung them open, and rooted around inside for her big leather-bound book of recipes.

She heaved it out and slammed it on the counter. This was where she kept every perfected recipe — some handed down from her grandmother, others she'd adapted or even created herself. Loose papers tucked between the pages, filled with hastily scrawled notes or measurements, stained here and there with splashes of vanilla extract or melted chocolate.

If she couldn't find something in here to beat Jassie's submission, she'd eat her apron.

Maeve paged through, frantically, all while the timer on the oven ticked away, and the scent of warm peanut butter filled the kitchen.

"No, not this," she muttered, flinging one page after another aside. "Definitely not that."

All of these recipes were delicious, but many would be nearly impossible to get right with vegan ingredients.

Her cell phone trilled from the living room, and she went to answer it, my mind whirring with possibilities. What about a triple-tiered vanilla cake with organic, cream-cheese frosting … no, wait, vegans didn't eat dairy, could she mimic cream cheese with—

"Hello?" she answered.

"Having a good evening?" Jassie's snark pinged in Maeve's ears, and any hope of having a good evening evaporated.

"How did you get this number?"

"Let's just say, I have my sources."

"What are you, the CIA?"

Jassie giggled, in that same breathy, girlish way she used to in high school. She'd sounded exactly like that on the night she'd been crowned prom queen. And again, right after she'd stolen Maeve's boyfriend.

"You're so funny. That's one of your two talents, Maeve. If only your other talent wasn't so … well, you know what they say, those who can't do, teach."

Maeve would've said *those who can't do pay others to do for them.* But she'd learned from experience that it was better to get conversations with Jassie over with fast. Any argument she started would just prolong the misery.

"What do you want, Jassie?"

"My, you're in a bad mood. You wouldn't happen to have been browsing my profile, would you?"

Maeve paced over to the foyer and up the stairs to the second floor. She had to move, or her pent-up nerves would erupt like lava through her teeth, and she'd end up saying something she'd regret later.

"Why are you calling?"

"I just wanted to find out how you were doing with your submission. You know you only have two days, right?"

"Thanks for the reminder."

"I really didn't expect you to go through with this whole thing. Considering how tough things have been for you, it might not be good for you. Mentally."

Maeve was sick of being toyed with. She cut straight to it. "What's your problem with me?"

Jassie sighed. "I have no idea what you're talking about — I thought we were friends. Having a friendly little competition."

Maeve hesitated. This was Jassie's trick. Being mean, then backtracking when someone called her on it. She loved pretending that *she* was the victim.

Maeve was done falling for it. "Whatever. I don't have

time for this. I've got cookies in the oven."

"Cookies? That's what you're making? Sounds like someone's never heard of making a good first—"

She hung up on Jassie, slammed her eyes shut, and drew a deep breath.

Jassie was trying to get to her, and Maeve wasn't going to let her. If she started second-guessing herself now, she'd still be trying to figure out what to bake while everyone else was handing in their entries.

Keeping it simple was still the smart move. The peanut butter cookies were only for qualifying; she'd come up with something more elaborate to serve the judges in the actual competition.

And if Jassie thought she was going to back out, she was going to be disappointed.

This was Maeve's dream. Not hers. Jassie could use her trust fund money to start her own bakery if she wanted to. She didn't need the prize money or the title. She just wanted to ruin Maeve's dreams.

The scent of something burning hit her nose. *The cookies.*

Maeve sprinted downstairs and darted into the kitchen. Smoke wisped through the cracks of the oven door and hung in the air above the burners.

She shoved the window open, switched on the stovetop fan, and whipped open the oven door. Smoke billowed out. She waved it away toward the window with her hand towel. The peanut butter cookies lay shriveled and black on the baking tray.

"You win this round, Jassie St. Clair," she growled.

Maeve dumped the charred cookies in the trash and the baking sheet into the kitchen sink. Then she brought a clean bowl out from under the counter and set to work on another batch.

If she had to, she'd stay up all night to get the cookies right.

Chapter Six

MAEVE BIT into another cookie from batch fifteen and chewed.

"Dry," she announced to her empty kitchen. "Dry as desert sand. Why can't I get this right?"

She dropped the cookie back onto the tray in disgust. Had she lost her touch over the last dozen hours?

Had Jassie cursed her with a case of bad juju?

Or was her palette ruined because she'd been tasting cookies all night?

At this point, Maeve wasn't sure if she could tell the difference between a cookie and a hockey puck.

"You're fine, it's fine." She ran crumby fingers over her batter-splashed apron. "Of course you're not fine. Look at you, for heaven's sake. You've made a million cookies and none of them are even edible. This is a disaster."

Twenty batches of cookies. One of which had been adapted from her grandmother's original recipe. The others were variations, some with added oatmeal or raisins. Both of which were superfoods, according to the internet.

She picked up a cookie from batch fourteen and bit into it.

Then spat it into the sink. Raisins and peanut butter? What had she been thinking?

The sun was barely up, but she'd already burned through three pots of coffee to keep herself conscious through the night. There was no chance of bed with the contest deadline looming. She still hadn't finished step one.

She turned toward the kitchen and blinked. Mom's garden was bright with colors: pink, yellow, violet, and red dotted through a mass of green. A lone butterfly drifted from flower to flower in one of the beds, mocking in its freedom.

Maeve trudged upstairs to her bedroom and grabbed her phone from where she'd tossed it on the bed.

She had five voicemails, a dozen additional texts, and a slew of notifications from BestGig, the freelancing app where new clients found her.

Every single message was from Leroy.

Where are you? It's been more than 12 hours since I texted you about the color palette.

I don't appreciate being ignored — you'd better be finishing the logo that I paid an extra $50 to expedite.

The final one, sent three minutes ago: *If I don't hear from you in the next hour, I'll be forced to leave a one-star review and register a complaint with BestGig. And I'll be finding another designer for future work.*

For six years she'd been producing high-quality graphics for Leroy, and he was ready to destroy her for being out of contact for — what, twenty-three hours?

Clients like Leroy were why she needed to win this contest.

None of her attempts had turned out as well as that first batch of cookies — the ones Baker had scarfed down.

But she had no idea how to make them better.

She had to get the samples to Emma. Her friend wasn't a baker, but her taste buds had never steered Maeve wrong.

Maeve separated the cookies into twenty different containers, labeling each with the batch number and ingredient list. (Batch number fourteen got a big red *X* on top: *here there be raisins.*)

She carted the containers out to her beat-up Honda and tucked them onto the backseat, in neat rows like lines of Tupperware soldiers.

After she got into the driver's seat, she looped her arm over the back of the passenger seat and made eye contact with her cookies.

"Some of you will live, and some of you will be eaten, and some of you, well, you should never have been created in the first place. I'm looking at you, number fourteen."

Motivational speech at an end, she reversed out of the driveway and made for Pretty Paws.

It was only when she'd made it to the locked door of the shelter with her leaning tower of containers that she realized it was barely past dawn, and Pretty Paws didn't open to the public until ten.

She grabbed her phone and called Emma.

"Good morning," she chirped on the second ring. Emma had always been a disturbingly-happy morning person.

"Hey, Em. You should let me in."

Through the windows on the front side, Maeve could just make out Emma turning around from whatever she'd been doing and noticing her on the other side of the glass.

Maeve smiled and held up one hand in a silent wave.

Emma rushed to the door and pushed it open. "What the...? Maeve? What are you doing?"

Maeve shifted under the precarious stack of Tupperwares. "I need help."

"Yeah, you do, but not the kind you think. Have you looked in the mirror this morning?" She stepped aside and waved Maeve into the lobby, so it was obviously alright.

Maeve started laying the containers out on the reception

desk. She still had her apron on, but she was well past the point of caring.

"You have cookie dough in your hair," Emma pointed out.

"Oh?" She reached up, and her fingers found a glob of dried-out dough in the hair at her temple. She sniffed it, curious. "Oof, Batch Three. Too much cinnamon."

Emma laughed, but the sound was strained. "What's going on?"

Maeve flicked the glob of Batch Three into the trashcan next to the desk and started pacing. Her new normal, apparently, the pacing.

"I've been baking all night." She walked toward the lobby chairs and back again. "All night, and I've got twenty batches of cookies done, right?"

"Holy … wow. All night? But the competition isn't for another week."

"The qualifying round is due tomorrow, remember? I told you about it yesterday."

"Dude, it's an audition. The cookies are meant to be edible. They don't have to be masterpieces."

Maeve stilled and pointed at her. "See, that's what they want you to think. But I know the truth. You have to make that first impression. What if I bake a batch of cookies that are too plain, and they punish me for it at the end?"

"It might not even be the same people judging the contest."

"Jassie made a double-tiered chocolate cake with coconut milk and natural sweeteners. And I bet it was the best thing they've ever had on their tongues. I can't let her get away with this."

"You need to sit down and take a breath." Emma took her by the shoulders and pushed her down into one of the little gray-upholstered waiting room chairs. "I'll get you a cup of coffee."

"Will you try my cookies?"

"Of course. Which one?"

"All of them. You have to tell me which one's the best. Except, well, fourteen. No one will like fourteen." Maeve frowned at the line of containers spreading across the receptionist desk. "Dunno why I brought that one."

"All twenty? I'm pretty sure that will turn me diabetic."

The door to the back of the shelter opened before Maeve could say anything else, and two people came into the lobby — Leslie, the cheerful woman who owned the shelter, and Dr. Dale, the pale, funny vet who helped run it.

"—don't think Athena will find a new home if she doesn't stop scratching all the time. Have we tried the venison?" Leslie broke off, spotting Maeve. She glanced toward the door as if looking for damage to the glass. "How'd you get in?"

"It's my fault, Les," Emma said. "This is my friend Maeve. She's going nuts."

Maeve frowned, but couldn't honestly disagree with the assessment.

Leslie gave Maeve an appraising look. "The Maeve from yesterday?"

"Yup."

A smiled sparkled in Leslie's dark eyes as she turned toward the receptionist desk and the row of cookies.

Dr. Dale had already wandered over to the desk and was examining the containers, lifting one off the desk. "What's with all the cookies?"

Maeve recognized the giant red X across the top of the one he held and leaped to her feet. "No, not those. That's Batch Fourteen. It's got raisins."

"Ah." He set the container back down, as carefully as if it were a grenade about to detonate.

"Maeve's going to join the HealthNut baking contest. This is her attempt at making a qualifying entry."

"They need this many different types?" Dr. Dale asked.

"Well, no." Maeve's cheeks got warm. It was one thing for Emma to think her crazy — it was an entirely different, and far worse, thing to give near-strangers the same impression. "I just wanted to get it perfect. But this is good. Now that you two are here, you can help me try them out."

"Sure," said Dr. Dale.

"I can't, unfortunately." Leslie patted her stomach where it pushed against her colorful scrubs. "Sugar before noon will have me sick all day."

"Okay. Then Dr. Dale and Emma can help me."

"Honey, you don't need this many options," Emma groaned. "You could bake a vanilla sponge cake and everyone would love it."

"I have to be sure." Maeve went over to the desk and opened the lid on Batch One, her grandmother's special recipe. She held the container out toward Dr. Dale. "My grammy's special peanut butter cookies, adapted to fit the HealthNut codes. They're vegan and—"

Dr. Dale withdrew his hand. "I'm sorry, I'm allergic to peanuts."

"Oh. Oh, no." Maeve shut the lid again, her shoulders sagging. She hadn't even thought about potential allergens. "I'm sorry. Are you okay?"

"Fine." He smiled warmly. "The hives only happen if I eat them."

Maeve deflated the rest of the way. The excitement that had carried her through the night was leaking out of her, fast. "I guess it's up to Emma."

"I want to help, but that many cookies? I could never."

Emma, too?

"What am I going to do?" Maeve pressed a hand to her forehead.

"I'm sure your cookies are great," Leslie said. "If they could convince the most antisocial dog in the shelter to jump on you, they'd have to be. Excuse us, ladies."

She headed for the door to the back, where the sound of barking dogs was coming from. Dr. Dale followed.

Maeve sighed and leaned her elbows on the reception desk, shutting her eyes for a moment. "Seriously, this is a disaster. What am I going to do?"

Emma pursed her lips. "You're really that desperate to have a taste tester?"

"I can't tell anymore which ones are good, if any of them are. What's a vegan cookie supposed to taste like, anyway?"

"I have an idea. But you have to promise me something. No, two somethings."

"Anything."

"Firstly," Emma said, raising a finger, "that you won't freak out. And secondly, that you'll take a shower before you go hand in your audition cookies."

"Done and done. What's the idea?"

"Why don't we get Baker to be the tester?" Emma asked.

"You're not seriously suggesting we feed that dog more cookies? I mean, yesterday was—"

"Not feed her, no. Especially not the raisin; raisins are toxic to dogs. But Baker clearly has a nose for them. I could bring her out now, and you could let her decide. See which ones she goes to first."

"That's ridiculous," Maeve said, her pulse ticking up a notch. She definitely wasn't prepared to be in the same room as a dog again. Especially not the dog who had jumped on her yesterday and started this whole re-baking debacle in the first place. "She's a dog."

"Dogs have the best sense of smell." Emma paused, narrowing her eyes. "Come on, Maeve. What have you got to lose?"

"Dog tastes are probably different from human tastes."

"Are you really going to let Jassie win, just because you're afraid of dogs?"

Maeve pictured Jassie's smug face when she found out that

she'd missed the deadline for submitting her entry. Jassie had distracted her last night, made her burn her second batch of cookies, and what if those were the winners? This was partly her fault.

"Fine," she said. "Let's see what the dog can do."

Chapter Seven

THE SMELL of cookies hovered around Emma as she crouched in front of Baker's cage, holding out a leash and smiling. "Come on, girl. I need your help."

She spoke in that soft, high voice that nice humans used a lot around dogs.

Not-nice humans shouted.

Baker stayed where she was, her back to the kennel wall. She didn't have to leave. She'd already been fed, and she was washed yesterday. But that smell…

Cookies.

Baker sniffed again, more insistently. She wagged her tail, once.

"That's right," Emma said. "Guess who's here? Maeve. And she's got more of those cookies."

Maeve was here.

Maeve, the human who was afraid. Baker was afraid of her, too. But she had cookies.

Slowly, she got to her feet and walked toward Emma. She allowed her to clip on the leash, then followed her down the long passage between the cages. A few of the dogs lay sleeping. Others barked and pushed against the fronts of their cages, their ears flapping. Naturally, Spotty-Ears was one of those.

One or two turned their heads this way and that, as if to ask if it was finally her turn to go to The Front.

Most dogs who went to The Front didn't come back, and those that did were sad, like they'd seen something strange and terrible up there. Baker's skin prickled at the thought. The Front was no place she ever wanted to go.

Near the end of the row, a big black dog sat with his nose pressed up against the wires of his kennel door. He bared his teeth and growled at Baker as she passed.

She didn't know what Emma and the other humans called him, but to her, his name was Bully. He hated her. He was the reason she wouldn't play in the yard — the first time she'd tried to go out, he'd been waiting. He chased her around and snapped at her legs.

The other humans had stopped him, and he wasn't allowed in the yard with other dogs anymore, only on his own. When they did take him out, he would growl as he passed by Baker's kennel.

Her hackles went up, but Bully didn't leap at the door. He simply watched.

Finally, they were out in the lobby, and the smell of cookies grew even stronger.

Baker drooled.

Maeve stepped back. She was covered in specks of cookie and smelled gooey and warm.

"Here she is," Emma said, and led her forward. "See? Baker's calm. She even came out of her cage willingly, and that's a first. All I had to say was the name 'Maeve' and she came out."

"Oh please, Em, I might be tired, but I'm not stupid. I highly doubt she even remembers me."

She wiped her hands on her cookie-speckled apron. It looked yummy. The type of thing Baker might dig her teeth into and sleep on, maybe at the same time.

"Sit, Baker," Emma said.

Baker sat down on the wooden floor and looked around. There were more of those clear boxes on the countertop.

Cookies!

Emma bent down to be eye-level with Baker. "We need your help. Maeve's made a bunch of cookies, but she can't decide which one's the best one. You can't eat them, but if you sniff them and tell us the best one, I can give you a treat."

She dropped the end of the leash, and Maeve took another step back, raising a protective hand.

Emma went to the desk and came back with a big jar. She opened it and showed Baker the bone-shaped treats inside. They didn't smell quite as good as the cookies, but her mouth still watered.

"You don't really think that dog can actually understand you?" Maeve shook her head. "This is really dumb. I can't believe I agreed to this."

"You're just afraid it will work."

"That's not what I'm afraid of at all."

"Are you ready, Baker?" Emma picked up one of the containers. "This is batch number one." She brought a box forward and opened it. "No eating. Just sniffing."

Baker licked her lips and teeth and sat very still. This was important. Maeve was scared, and if she could help Maeve feel less frightened, that was good. She'd felt scared so often, and it was a terrible thing to feel.

"Here." Emma placed the box under her nose.

Baker sniffed, and the scent exploded in her nostrils. Soft, warm and delicious. Gooey and peanut buttery. She wagged her tail to let Emma know this was a very good one. It smelled exactly like the cookies she'd eaten yesterday.

"She's wagging her tail. She likes it!" Emma grinned over her shoulder at Maeve.

Maeve peered down at Baker, lowered her hand and took

a step forward. "The ones based on my grammy's old recipe. But it's probably a fluke. She'll probably wag her tail for all of them."

Her lips peeled back over her teeth and her forehead went wrinkly.

Emma came back with a second box. "What about this one, girl?"

Baker looked up at Maeve. She wasn't as scared anymore, but having the humans this close made her skin tingle. What if she barked and they got angry? What if they shouted or hit her?

"You can do it, Baker. Maeve, say something encouraging."

Maeve's cheeks went pink like the underside of a puppy's paws. "Yes, Baker, go ahead. You're a good girl."

Good girl. She hadn't heard those words in a very long time. Not since before Michael.

She sniffed the box and choked on the smell. She turned her head away.

"Would you look at that? I told you this would work." Emma fetched a doggy bone treat out of the jar on the desk and set it on the floor.

Baker gobbled it up, crunching it between her teeth. It was delicious, and helped get the smell of the bad cookies out of her nose.

"Let's try the others." Emma winked at Maeve.

Box after box came, and Baker sniffed each one, turning her head when it smelled gross or wagging her tail if it was okay. Emma gave her a treat every three boxes. It was a fun game, and Maeve seemed to like it, too — at least, she crept a little forward with each box until she was almost close enough to stroke Baker's head.

"I think she likes number one the best," Emma said. "That or number thirteen. Here girl. Which one is your favorite?"

Baker considered both boxes. They were both yummy, but the first one was the best of the lot. She hopped up to her feet and wagged her tail at the first box.

"See? She likes number one! This is your cookie for the competition."

Maeve took the box back from Emma.

Baker blinked up at her, and she stared back. Then she said, "Thanks."

Baker dared to bark. Just a little, not to be frightening, but to be happy.

And Maeve didn't yell, or back away, or even leave. She sat on the sofa with a sigh. "That's something, at least."

"See? All's well that ends well. But you forgot to do one last thing." Emma walked to Maeve and gave her the big container of doggy treats. It had marks on its sides that looked like the prints dogs left behind in the mud after it rained.

"What?" Maeve asked.

"You have to give Baker a treat."

Chapter Eight

"Whoa there," Maeve said, staring at the ceramic container of Milk-Bones. "Let's not get ahead of ourselves."

"She won't bite you." Emma smiled, like that would help. "Has she seemed aggressive at all since she came in here? No. Did she tell you which batch of cookies was the best? Yes. You have nothing to worry about."

Maeve licked her lips, her heart throbbing in her ears. What if Baker decided her fingers looked tastier than the treats? Or what if she…?

"Maeve. She's a sweetheart. Look at her."

Baker sat still in the reception area, right next to the coffee table. She didn't wag her tail or make a noise; she simply watched, her head tilted to one side and one ear flopping up. She was actually kind of pretty.

In short, any person who hadn't been viciously mauled by a dog as a child would have found her adorable. Not Maeve, though. That melty feeling around her heart was a symptom of exhaustion, not affection.

"Go ahead." Emma rattled the Milk-Bones. "She deserves a reward. You'll like petting her again."

Maeve sighed, resigned, took a biscuit from the container, and walked over to Baker.

The dog wagged her tail once.

"Here," she said, holding the biscuit out toward Baker. Somehow, being so close to the dog was even scarier than the day before. Maybe because she had a choice this time, and she was doing it even though she knew better.

Baker took the treat gingerly from between her fingers and crunched it up, wagging her tail a second time. Maeve stretched out her hand, hesitantly. She sniffed it. No licking, thank goodness — she was not ready for mouth-to-hand contact.

Maeve patted her on the head, real slow. She was solid, but soft at the same time.

"Good girl." The words felt kind of weird.

Baker wagged her tail again.

Maeve backed away and sat back on the sofa, relieved to be out of biting range again. "There. I did it."

"Good girl." Emma grinned, and closed the treats. She set it back behind the counter, then took hold of Baker's leash and held it loosely at her side. "Because I've been thinking about something."

"Uh oh." Maeve swiped the hair back from her forehead. She was toast. She needed a shower, some time to relax, and maybe an entire day of sleep. But she couldn't avoid Leroy for much longer, and she had a class to teach today. "What is it?"

"Baker's clearly got a gift for sniffing out delicious food. I'm not saying you should take her home or anything, but you should definitely come back and see her."

"See her?" Maeve frowned. "Em, I told you I'm not interested in getting a dog."

"For sure, but she's obviously good at picking out great food. You should come back to the shelter every time you've made something for the contest and let her test it. Give it the old snifferoo."

"Snifferoo?"

"It's a word." Emma laughed. "Come on, it'll be good for both of you. And who knows? Baker might be your secret to success in the upcoming competition. A way to beat Jassie."

"We both know that's ludicrous."

"You know what's even more ludicrous? The fact that I'm not letting you leave the shelter until you agree to come back and see Baker. She's never opened up to anyone like—"

"Em, I can't—"

"I'll make you feed her another treat. Don't think I won't do it."

Maeve didn't have the energy left to fight. "Fine. But I still think it's crazy. And I'm not taking her home."

"Deal." Emma's grin was far too excited.

Maeve didn't have the heart to let her down. Truth was, she didn't plan on opening her home to anyone, ever again, human or animal. She'd learned her lesson.

All she cared about was winning the money to start her bakery.

Chapter Nine

Maeve took a breath and unlocked her front door, the morning sun on her back. She'd done it. She'd woken up early this morning to bake another batch of her grandmother's cookies. Now, they waited at the college for a HealthNut representative to pick them up.

What if they weren't good enough? She'd bet her dream on stray dog's sniffer.

"Baker, you'd better be right," she muttered as she set her tote on the foyer table and walked through to the living room. The TV was off, the curtains were drawn, and her laptop was waiting.

It had been almost forty-eight hours since Leroy first messaged her about changing the shade of green in his image. Sometime during the night, he'd gone ominously silent.

Maeve was half-afraid to log in and see whether he'd lodged the complaint and left the one-star review that he'd threatened.

But she half-hoped that he had, and that she'd never have to deal with him again.

Instead, she found that her BestGig account had been

suspended, pending investigation of a client complaint of fraudulent activity. No further explanation.

Leroy.

Okay, so she'd been ghosting him for two days, not interested in his "graphic design emergency" while she was trying to figure out her entry for the HeathNut competition. But accusing her of fraud? That was an absurd overreaction.

As long as her account was suspended, she not only couldn't finish the job for Leroy, she also couldn't take on any other jobs, from existing clients or new ones. He was trying to cut her off entirely from her main source of income, and that was far worse than anything she'd ever done to him.

Deep breath. Maeve followed her own advice and sucked in air through her teeth. She hadn't committed fraud. BestGig would recognize that.

She sent an email to their help desk, requesting information about the complaint, and immediately received an autoresponder message saying they replied to queries in the order received, and that she should wait forty-eight hours before contacting them again. In the meantime, all her existing clients would see her suspended profile and that unfair fraud accusation.

She groaned. Past experience suggested she would be contacting them again — they were quick to respond to client issues, but slower to deal with freelancer complaints.

But her only option was to wait. Or maybe she could email or text any customers who'd contacted her outside of BestGig.

Starting with an apology to Leroy. He might withdraw the complaint if she made nice.

An hour later, she'd contacted everyone she could, letting them know that there'd been a glitch at BestGig and that it would be fixed soon. If they had any work for her in the meantime, she'd be happy to help them.

Mom used to say that thing about a watched pot never

boiling, which Maeve always thought was ridiculous, because of course water boiled at the same rate whether someone watched or not. It just felt like it'd never get there.

It was perfect description of her life: standing around, waiting for things to finally heat up.

She strode to the curtains and dragged them open, letting the sun's rays into the living room. Then she opened the windows as well.

A meow broke the silence.

She peered out the window, into the flowerbed below.

Macavity, the neighbor's cat, sat in the garden, peering up at her. Mrs. Johnston had adopted him about three weeks ago, but he spent more time at Maeve's house than at hers.

"What now? You know I can't feed you."

Macavity leapt onto the windowsill and purred his way into the living room. Maeve didn't mind cats, and as they went, he was about the cutest. Mrs. Johnston had named him after her favorite character in the *Cats* musical, because he was both mysterious and criminally-inclined.

Later, she'd discovered he was also mean to the neighborhood dogs, but he liked Maeve, so she stroked him and let him take a seat on the sofa. He licked the fiddly front bit of his chest, sticking his tongue out in that obscene way cats liked to do, then curled into a ball in the sunshine.

Ah, the life of a cat. A part of her wished she could be like Macavity. Live the simple life and let somebody else worry about all the stressful stuff.

She sighed and pinched the bridge of her nose.

Her cell trilled from her bag in the hall. What if it was the HealthNut people, calling to tell me that she'd made it into the competition? She ran to grab it.

"Hello?" No one answered. "Hello?"

"Just a sec!" Emma's voice crackled through the phone. "I —oops!"

"What?"

"Hi," she said, clearing up again. "Sorry about that. How are you today?"

There was a strange tone to Emma's voice. Something Maeve couldn't quite place. "Okay, how are you? And why are you calling?"

"What, a friend can't call another friend anymore? That's harsh."

"Not like that, I just … I thought you were volunteering at the shelter today."

"Oh, I am. I mean, I was." Emma chuckled. "I've just got a surprise for you."

"You do?"

"Yeah. Just one sec." A door slammed in the background, and she whispered something Maeve couldn't make out. "Okay, back."

"What's going on?"

"Nothing, nothing, all part of the surprise."

Maeve frowned. "All right. So, what is this surprise?"

"Well, you know how you've been really down lately? Super-sarcastic and weird, and how you spent all night baking twenty batches of cookies for a baking contest audition?"

"Don't spare my feelings or anything."

"You know what I mean. You've been really down and out lately. I just want you to cheer up. And I think I've found the way to do that."

"You'd better not be setting me up on a date, because that is the last thing I want or need."

"Not quite." Emma's voice trembled with barely-contained excitement. "Come to the front door."

"Huh?"

"Come outside!"

Maeve walked over and opened the front door.

• • •

EMMA STOOD ON THE PORCH, grinning and tucking her phone into the pocket of her jeans. She held a leash in her other hand. On the end of the leash was Baker, the boxer with a nose for Maeve's cookies.

Baker looked up with soft brown eyes, and that weird melty sensation around Maeve's heart came back.

Strange, because she'd gotten plenty of sleep last night.

"What are you doing here?" she asked.

"Surprise!" Emma held out the end of the leash. "I brought you a present."

"Did you hide it somewhere in the dog?"

"That's ... I don't want to know what you mean by that."

"To be honest, I'm not even sure. But why have you brought her here?"

"Because you're going to keep her for a while."

"I think I'm not." Emma opened her mouth again, but before she could argue, Maeve added, "No, I am definitely sure that's not happening."

Baker planted her furry butt on the porch. Maeve kept a wary eye on her, in case she decided to growl, or bare her teeth, or mistake her for a peanut butter cookie.

She didn't move.

"Hear me out." Emma lifted her palm. "So, you know how Pretty Paws is a no-kill shelter?"

"Yeah."

"What you probably don't know is that we've really been struggling lately. As in, there's not really enough money to go around and the more doggy mouths to feed, the worse it gets." Emma dragged her teeth over her bottom lip. "Leslie needs the space, and if Baker doesn't leave, then she might have to go to another shelter."

"Oh?"

"So. The only other shelter in the area is ... well, the opposite of a no-kill."

"Oh." The melty feeling got meltier. And sadder. She pushed it down. "What's that got to do with me?"

"Well, I figured if she gets a few weeks of fostering, then maybe she might make some progress. Because there's someone paying more attention to her, yeah? Then she could come back to Pretty Paws with a better chance of getting adopted. Basically, she just needs a place to stay. And since my apartment complex has a no-pets rule, I figured…"

"Absolutely not. You know how I feel about dogs."

"Baker's sweet. She'd never bite you, or even growl—"

"The very first time she saw me, she practically knocked me over."

"With enthusiasm. She wasn't trying to hurt you."

"But she still could have."

"Look at how awesome she was at identifying which cookies you should make for the competition. You can use her natural talents for figuring out what product you want to present to HealthNut."

She had to be kidding. "There's got to be somebody else who can take her."

"There isn't," Emma said, firmly. "If you don't take her, just for a week or two, Baker's going to wind up at a shelter that's not nearly as willing to put in the effort as Pretty Paws. She could be put down. Could you really let that happen to her?"

"But I don't even — I don't know how to look after a dog."

"You feed them, give them water, and let them sleep on a blanket or something. It's not that hard."

"Speak for yourself," Maeve grumbled.

"So, that's a yes? You'll watch her for a few weeks? She can help you with your baking competition and everything."

It was a lame excuse — did Emma really believe Baker had picked the right cookies?

Did Maeve?

She looked down at Baker again, and wondered if she could live with herself if the dog got sent to a shelter that would put her down.

"Fine," she said, at last.

Emma squealed with joy and practically bowled her over as she led Baker into the house. Maeve hesitated, pulse pounding in her throat. It was one thing to run into the dog at the shelter, but having her in the house?

Being alone with her? No one else around to pull her off her if she attacked?

Her palms were slick with sweat. She shut the front door and entered the living room, where Emma had already sat on the sofa. Macavity had taken his exit — he wasn't dumb enough to stick around to find out if Baker was friendly.

Baker sat on her hind legs, paws planted on the floor, watching Maeve as she crossed to the other side of the room and stood near the windows.

"See, this is nice." Emma smiled.

"Okay. I guess. But you have to stay here for a while. Maybe you could sleep over?"

"Maeve, you're not seriously afraid of her."

"What if she rips my face off the minute you leave?"

"Everything's going to be fine, trust me. You're doing a great thing by taking her in like this. She would've had nowhere else to go. Isn't that right, Baker?"

The dog settled down on all fours and rested its head on its legs.

"See? Look how sweet she is. Wouldn't hurt a fly."

Maeve didn't trust that for a second. "You have to stay."

"I can't. I have to get back to the shelter, and don't you have work to do?"

She didn't want to get into the story of how Leroy might've torpedoed her design career. "So much, I might be too busy to take care of a dog."

"Baker will be great company. She's a sweetie, and you're

going to fall in love with her." Emma sounded like she was trying to convince herself as much as Maeve.

"Em—"

"I'll see you later." She unclipped the leash, rolled it up, and handed it to Maeve, then turned back toward the front door.

"Emma!"

But she was already gone. The door clicked closed behind her, and a car started outside a moment later.

Maeve stared at Baker, and the dog stared back.

"Don't make any sudden movements," she whispered to herself. "She won't attack if you don't move too much."

Maeve scooched along the far end of the room, slowly, as she tried to figure out how she was going to get through the next couple of weeks.

She didn't have dog food, but was it a good idea to leave Baker alone in the house while she went shopping?

What if she wouldn't let her put the leash back on

Didn't you have to walk dogs every day?

And how was she going to come up with a prize-winning recipe for the competition when she had to tiptoe around Baker to keep her from attacking her?

How had Emma manipulated her into this?

Baker's dark-eyed gaze followed Maeve as crept through the living room. "Slow and steady wins the race."

Once she made it to the hall and the base of the staircase, she ran all the way up to her bedroom and slammed the door behind her, panting and shaking.

She was trapped.

Chapter Ten

MAEVE'S PLACE smelled a lot better than the shelter, and it looked better, too. There weren't any other dogs here, and it was quiet, except for the chirping of birds outside the window.

Baker sprawled out on the cool wooden floor, her head on her paws. The wooden legs of a small table sat in front of her nose. Two comfy chairs with fat, puffy cushions filled the room. The faint smell of cookies drifted on the air, but the far sharper scent from Maeve was there, too.

Fear.

She was afraid.

It was a strange, for a human to be afraid of Baker. It made her insides feel cold — she was the one who had always been scared of them.

But, apart from the sharp smell of fear, this place wasn't so bad.

And Maeve didn't seem so bad either. She didn't want to come near Baker at all. She couldn't hurt her if she wasn't close. Which was safe.

She'd gone up the wooden steps, and now she was over-head, stomping around.

"—got to be crazy to be doing this!" Her voice was all squeaky and high, like a yelp but with words.

Baker lifted her ears.

"Emma, hello? Yeah. You've got to come back, right now. I can't do this."

Maeve didn't want her here, but that was fine. Baker didn't want to be here either. She didn't want to be anywhere with humans. Maybe if they went for a walk, Baker could run away … but no, she'd tried that once and a man in a van came and put a rope around her neck. He'd taken her to a terrible shelter — she'd barely gotten out of there alive.

"No, no, no, you don't understand. I just can't do it. She's — Emma. Emma? Hello?" A thump. "You've got to be kidding me."

Then Maeve fell quiet, apart from the pacing.

Baker listened for a while, a whine building in her chest. She swallowed it down.

Poor Maeve. She was so afraid, but if she stayed up there, Baker couldn't show her that she didn't want to bite her.

On the other hand, if she didn't come back down, she couldn't shout or kick. So maybe it was better this way.

A soft rustle from outside drew Baker's attention. She walked to the window and rested her nose on the sill. Outside, it smelled of flowers and green grass and…

Saliva and fish?

A cat leapt onto the windowsill and turned around, presenting its rear end to Baker's face.

She would've sniffed, if it had been a dog. But cats weren't any better than humans. They'd scratch your nose and steal your food first chance they got. She'd learned that the hard way when she was knocking over garbage cans to find scraps to eat.

Baker retreated.

The cat turned and hissed, flashing sharp white fangs.

One of her owners had also had a cat who she'd loved

much more than she'd loved Baker. The furry black hellion had hated her, and she'd stayed away from it.

What are you doing here? this cat's stiffly-raised tail seemed to say. *This is my turf.*

Baker turned her back on it. *I don't care if it's your turf or not. I'm here now.*

She didn't want this cat thinking it had the advantage. They were like that, thinking they owned everything. Well, this one didn't own her.

The cat stretched upward and stuck its claws into the wooden side of the window. It scratched, peeling away flakes of paint and polish. *Maeve is mine!*

A low growl started up in my throat. *You don't own the human.*

That's what you think. The cat turned and pressed its hindquarters up against the wood, getting ready to mark it. *Watch this.*

Baker barked warningly. *Don't you dare!*

The cat stepped away. It hadn't sprayed the windowsill, but it hissed again as footsteps thundered down the wooden stairs that Maeve had climbed earlier.

This isn't over. Then the cat leapt out of the window, into the garden, and was gone.

Maeve appeared under the big white arch. She had her fists on her hips, and her forehead was wrinkly. This was it. The shouting was about to start.

Baker crouched to the floor, bracing herself for a kick.

But the human didn't point her finger at Baker and scream, or fetch a stick or anything. Instead she sighed and looked toward the open window.

"What happened?" she asked. "No, no, it doesn't matter. Okay. Wait. You need food, right? And water. And something to sleep on. Wait here. Don't move."

Then she went back upstairs.

Baker waited, her nose itching at the horrible fish-and-spit smell of that cat.

Maeve returned, carrying a big fluffy blanket in her arms.

"Come on. This way." Then she set off down the hall.

Baker padded after her. She wasn't shouting, but what if she was taking her outside? Once, after she'd chewed up a sock, she'd been tied up in the dark and cold for days without food or water. She'd been so thirsty, she licked dew off the grass each morning, everywhere the chain would reach.

But Maeve didn't lead her outside. Instead, she opened a door that split into two pieces, a bottom and a top. A bowl of water had been placed on the tiled floor, next to another one with bits of shredded meat in it.

Baker's stomach grumbled at the sight. It hadn't been too long since she'd eaten, but this smelled amazing. She hurried into the room.

Maeve stood outside the door, ready to run. She put the blanket on the floor, then shut the bottom half of the door and fiddled with the latch until it clicked into place.

"This is where you'll stay. For now. I'll let you out into the garden later to do your stuff in a little bit. You know what I mean. What am I talking about? Of course, you don't know what I mean." She backed up a step or two. "You'll be fine here."

Then she turned and hurried off.

The room smelled a lot like clean things. There was a big white machine with a window on the front in one corner, and lots of shelves too high to reach.

This was … fine. Nice, even. Much better than listening to other dogs barking or growling all day, or having strange humans come in and stare at her, deciding if they wanted to take her somewhere else.

Who knew how long it would last? She might as well enjoy it while she could.

Baker went over to the bowl of food and started to eat.

Chapter Eleven

Putting Baker in the laundry room helped. It was easier for Maeve to believe she was safe with a firm door between them, even though she would have to let her out sometime, and she could always bite her then. At least she'd be on her guard then, and, for now, she could relax.

She set her laptop on the kitchen counter and checked her email. No response from BestGig. No response to her effusive apology from Leroy, either. Or from any of her other clients.

She had no paying work to do, so she toyed with the idea of finishing Leroy's job and sending it to him for approval — maybe if he got what he wanted, he'd retract his complaint?

But the idea of spending more time on a job that she might never get paid for, to suck up to a client who'd been a total pain from the beginning, after she'd already groveled for his forgiveness ... *no way.*

Not when she could use that same time to perfect a recipe that might make her dreams come true.

Speaking of which, she still hadn't gotten an email from HealthNut about her entry.

How long did it take to decide if a cookie tasted edible?

She sighed, tugged her apron strings tighter, and braced

her palms on the counter. It was still morning and she had a whole day ahead of her, but she couldn't find the energy to put on a smile and continue on like everything was A-OK.

Not that it mattered. Because that was exactly what she had to do.

This is your shot. Don't forget that.

Assuming she made the first cut.

She squeezed her eyes shut and took a breath. *It will work out. You've got this.*

Besides, thinking about the contest was less scary than thinking about the fact that she still had to figure out how she was going to take care of a dog for the next two weeks.

She opened her eyes and found a new email in her inbox.

HealthNut Healthy Sweet Product Line Entry.

Maeve's heart did about twenty backflips and stuck the landing between her ribs.

She clicked on it, her finger slipping on the mousepad.

Congratulations! You've made it past the audition phase of the HealthNut Healthy Sweet Product Line Competition.

So, what's next?

The final competition will take place next Friday. All you need to do is come up with your perfect HealthNut Healthy Sweet Product and arrive at the front desk with the following number to check in.

Contestant 987

Congratulations on making it in. We can't wait to see what you bake up!

Regards,

The HealthNut Team

She read the email three times, her throat closing up.

She'd made it.

She'd thought she could, but a part of must've not been entirely sure, because the relief was so intense, she felt dizzy.

HealthNut thought her gluten-free, vegan peanut butter cookies were good enough.

She still had a shot at her dream.

Take that, Jassie.

Glee erupted. She shrieked and jumped on the spot, flinging her arms into the air.

Baker barked and popped up from behind the half-door leading into the laundry room. She stuck her snout over it and whined.

"Sorry. I mean, I'm fine. It's all great."

Was she seriously talking to a dog, right now? Instead of continuing that craziness, she grabbed her cell phone from the counter and dialed Emma's number.

It rang twice before she answered. "Hello?"

"I got in!" Maeve yelled.

Baker barked again.

She danced around in a circle, waving one hand in the air. "I got in. I can't believe it. I seriously got in."

"Got in where?"

"The competition. I passed the audition. I'm in the main event next week."

"Of course you are," Emma said, like it had been a foregone conclusion. "Have you tasted your cookies? They're amazing."

"This is it, Em. Oh gosh, now I have to figure out what I'm actually going to make for the main event. Oh wow."

"Make more cookies. They were a hit with Baker."

"I can't make cookies. That's like … trust me, everyone's going to be making cookies. I have to think of something better than that. I'll call you later, I've got to get to work. This is just the biggest deal ever and I wanted you to know."

"Good luck," Emma said, laughing as she hung up.

Maeve put the phone down, smiling. Not even the fact that Baker was still hanging onto the laundry room door could get her down.

"Now," she said, speaking to herself, definitely not to the dog. Of course, not to the dog. Why would she talk to the dog? "Where's my recipe book?"

Maeve walked to the long cupboard next to the fridge and opened the door. This was where she kept her collection — baking recipes and cookbooks were her favorite things to collect. But her all-time favorite book was the leather-bound volume.

She scanned the row of precariously stacked books and frowned. She didn't see it.

Weird. Usually, she could spot it from a mile away.

Had she left it in the living room? She peered past the cupboard and into the open-plan living area. Nothing there except her empty coffee mug from earlier. She frowned harder.

She grabbed the books and brought them out onto the counter, one by one. She stacked them in piles, just to be certain, until there was nothing left in the cupboard but a few loose papers containing old cupcake recipes and a grocery list.

"This can't be happening."

These books were great, but she needed her secret weapon to beat Jassie: her grandmother's recipes. She was already handicapped by the fact that her final entry had to be vegan. There was no way she'd be able to whip up something unique without her special recipes.

Maeve tried not to panic.

"It's going to be okay," she said, hoping hearing the words aloud would make them more believable.

Baker whined, and Maeve glanced over at her, meeting her dark-eyed gaze. She lifted her nose and sniffed.

"What? Are you hungry?"

But she'd fed her earlier, and her Googling told her that overfeeding a dog was a big no-no.

Maybe she had poop?

Baker didn't claw at the door, but rested her head on her paws atop it.

"Okay, then. You good?"

Again, no whine or bark.

She seemed fine, and this was an emergency. Maeve's future bakery was on the line.

She re-stacked the recipe books in the cupboard, her heart rate climbing with each passing moment. As she put each book back, she double-checked to make sure she hadn't mistaken the leather-bound book for another.

But no. It just wasn't there.

Maeve went through the other cupboards.

Not there either.

She even checked the fridge, just in case — she'd once put her shoe in the freezer by accident. Thankfully, she'd realized her ready meal wasn't meant to go on her foot before trying to slip her toes into frozen mac 'n cheese.

But the recipe book wasn't there.

She usually kept it in the cupboard. She'd made a habit of returning it specifically because of the whole shoe-in-the-freezer incident.

She did another check of the cupboard. But it still wasn't there.

She stalked into the living room.

"Where was I when I had it last?" She'd used it when she'd been making all those the cookies, but she couldn't for the life of her remember where she'd put it. She'd been so sleep-deprived by the time she took batch number twenty out of the oven, she could've left it anywhere.

Oh God, not the oven. Imagining the precious book charred beyond recognition, she bolted to the kitchen and yanked open the oven door. Empty. *Hallelujah.*

She dashed upstairs and checked in her bedroom, threw her drawers and closet open, even lowered herself to the carpet and peered under her bed. Nothing, except a sock she thought had crawled into the drier last week, only to be sucked into the missing socks vortex.

"Where is it?" she squeaked.

Okay, relax. This is not the end of the world.

Baker barked downstairs, and her frustration bubbled over. If she didn't need to go out and she'd just eaten, what could the dog possibly want?

What if Maeve couldn't figure it out, and Baker got frustrated, too? Frustrated enough to bite?

She grunted, got up, and hurried downstairs.

Baker hopped a few times as soon as she saw her and pressed her paws against the door, her ears flopping. If it wasn't for all those teeth, she'd be kind of cute.

"What? I'm kind of in the middle of a crisis here. Can't you wait to bite me until later?"

She barked again, and Maeve sighed. The dog probably needed the bathroom, and she couldn't hold that against her.

"Fine. But let's make this quick, okay? I've got major problems right now. I can't find my book."

When Maeve came forward, Baker immediately jumped off the door and backed up, wagging her furry butt but not her tail.

She drew back the bottom latch of the door, almost forgetting to feel afraid.

As soon as she started forward, though, the fear came screaming back. Maeve hurried away from the laundry room door, terror building in my throat. She swallowed, forced herself to woman up, and headed for the back door. She unlocked it and waited, holding it for the dog.

But Baker didn't come running out to pee. Or even to attack. Instead, she trotted from the laundry room toward the living room.

"Hey," Maeve called. "What are you doing?"

The end of her tail disappeared around the corner.

Maybe she found the living room carpet more comfortable? But no, she had a fluffy blanket. What kind of fussy dog had Emma saddled her with?

Maeve shut the back door and followed Baker cautiously, in case it was a trap — some doggy trick to draw her into a false sense of security. She could just imagine the horror movie playing out. Maeve entering the living room, Baker waiting, maybe even wagging her tail to set her at ease before it was Cujo time.

You're so dramatic, scolded a voice in the back of Maeve's head. She entered the living room.

Baker was waiting, all right, but instead of pouncing, she sniffed and pawed at the couch cushions, whining.

"Hey, don't do that. That's … you're going to break it. Or, I don't know, tear it?"

But the dog wouldn't let up. She snuffled and pawed, then whined and looked up at her with those puppy dog eyes.

"What is it? I don't get—" The words died on her lips. The corner of a leather-bound book poked out from underneath the cushion. "No way. Is that—?"

Maeve strode toward the sofa, and Baker backed up, lowering her hindquarters, her tail tucking between her legs.

No fast movements, remember?

She forced herself to walk the rest of the way to the couch in slow motion.

"Is that my book?"

Baker sat.

Maeve kept her eyes on Baker, in case she planned to lunge for her jugular or something, as she reached under the cushion and pulled out the book. She nearly drowned in relief. Baker had found her secret weapon.

But that had to be a coincidence. It wasn't like she could understand her, and even if she could, how would she know which book she was looking for?

Even so, her heart still wanted to melt. This time, with something like gratitude.

"How did you know that was there? Did you smell it out or something?"

There was a splotch of peanut butter on the pages from her baking all-nighter, the latest addition to the chocolate smears and butter stains the book had sustained over the years.

Baker had followed her nose to the scent that reminded her of cookies. She definitely didn't hear her say she'd lost her book and find it for her.

Maeve wasn't sure how her secret weapon had ended up under the couch cushions, but sleep deprivation can make a person do crazy things, right?

Or forget why they did perfectly reasonable-at-the-time things.

She tucked the book against her chest, stroking the spine with her fingers.

"Thank you," she said, then shook her head. Talking to a dog. It was ridiculous. Baker couldn't understand. "Okay, do you need to go outside?"

There she went again, talking to the dog like she could understand her.

Baker got up and paced toward the kitchen.

"Hey! Where are you going?"

Her claws clicked across the tiles, then she disappeared through the doorway.

Maeve followed her slowly, ninja-walking and peeking around corners just in case. But Baker wasn't in the kitchen.

"What—?" She placed the recipe book on the counter.

Baker sat on her blanket in the laundry room across the hall, watching her.

Maybe she needed space, too. Unexpected, but kind of refreshing. David had been needy all the time, constantly bugging Maeve for attention, even when she was obviously working.

Who'd have thought a dog would turn out to be more self-reliant than a boyfriend?

And she had helped. If Maeve told David that she'd lost her recipe book, he'd have tried to turn that into a reason she should spend more time with him instead of wasting her time baking.

The dog laid down on her blanket, crossed her paws, and rested her head on them, like they were having a slumber party and she was waiting for Maeve to start dishing about something.

Even though there was still no way she'd ever adopt a dog, Maeve had to admit she was *kinda* cute.

And she clearly had a good nose, at least for organic peanut butter.

"Thanks," she repeated, tapping her fingers on the leather cover. "But just so we're clear, you're not staying. Not for longer than Emma needs you here. Got it?"

Baker didn't bark or whine. She just looked at Maeve like she was wondering what she would do next.

She was used to being locked up in a cage at the shelter. Emma took her out for exercise every day, but even so, three months is a long time to be stuck in a box. That had to be depressing.

It would drive Maeve nuts, not being able to pace.

Her laundry room was bigger, with a bit of room to maneuver, but with the door closed, it was a different kind of cage.

She'd be going back to that after she left here, probably for months. To hear Emma tell it, Baker was unadoptable because she was so afraid of people. How awful would that be, terrified of everyone but forced to depend on their kindness?

Poor Baker.

"Would you like me to leave the door open, so you can walk around a little?" Maeve felt like an idiot for asking, and a jerk for not asking sooner.

Baker looked at her for a moment. Then she got up, grabbed the blanket in her mouth, and dragged it into the kitchen, where she dropped it in the far corner — as far as she could get from Maeve and still be in the kitchen.

Then she looked up at her while keeping her head low, as if requesting permission to be there.

"I can be good if you can," Maeve said.

Baker wagged her tail, then turned in a circle twice and lay on the blanket, again resting her head on her crossed paws.

Maybe she was so used to being in a cage that she thought she had to lie down.

That made Maeve kind of sad — if it made her feel better to lie down in a bigger space, she could be brave enough to give Baker a chance to prove she didn't need to be locked in the laundry room.

At least she could give her enough freedom to pace a bit before she had to go back to living in a cage.

Just for a while.

Okay, the contest. What could Maeve make to beat Jassie?

Something gluten-free, animal product-free, and allergen-free?

Something that tasted delicious, but that literally everyone could eat, no matter how health-conscious they were?

She chose three recipes to experiment with.

Brownies — because they would be easy to mass produce.

Mini-roly poly cakes covered in vanilla frosting, because if she could make those taste right, they'd be a home run.

And raspberry custard cups with a crispy crust.

Thankfully, she'd stocked up on vegan-friendly ingredients during her rampage the day before. She had everything she needed to get started on all three. Even tapioca flour and glucomannan fiber for thickening the egg-free custard.

Maeve set to work, hurrying back and forth in the kitchen, clanking pots and pans into place on the stovetop, heating up the oven, bringing out bowls and measuring ingredients.

When she added coconut flour and potato starch to the brownie batter in the electric mixer and it poofed some of the fine powders back at her, Baker let out a soft bark.

"I hope you're not laughing at me," she said.

Baker wagged her tail once.

That was something. A tail-wag that didn't involve food.

"All right," Maeve said, "so, now we have to reduce the raspberries. We can use pectin or agar, those are both vegan. Which do you think we should try first, Baker?"

Talking to her was silly, but Baker wagged her tail anyway.

It had been a long while since Maeve had someone in the house to talk to. Even Emma didn't have the patience to hang out with her when she was baking.

It was nice. Not maybe-she-would-adopt-a-dog nice, but she didn't mind Baker being there, for the first time since Emma had dumped her in the house.

"All right, let's look it up and see which one's healthier. We want to make the healthiest dessert, right?" Maeve pulled up Google. "It seems like they're about the same, and the recipe already calls for pectin."

Baker lifted her snout, gave her another wag of the tail.

"Okay that's settled. Now I need to figure out the best way to sweeten the raspberries."

She'd gone a little crazy at the grocery store: brown rice syrup, coconut sugar, unrefined maple syrup, organic sugar, and something called monk fruit extract that was supposed to come from a super-sweet cucumber-like plant that grew some-where in Asia. She'd even made a point to buy organic beet sugar to use in small quantities, because she'd read that some vegans wouldn't eat cane sugar that had been bleached with charred bones, which was apparently the norm. *Yuck.*

She'd ruled out agave syrup, because some people said it was so high in fructose that it was better to eat regular sugar, and stevia extract, which was plant-based and calorie-free, but also had a licorice aftertaste that Maeve didn't want anywhere near her treats.

Erythritol and xylitol were both out of the question. They were supposed to be healthy, but some people had a bad reaction. Like, diarrhea-bad. She wasn't taking a chance that the HealthNut judge might think her treat had given him food poisoning.

"What if we start with the least-processed stuff first?" she asked Baker. "Coconut nectar and unrefined maple syrup?"

Baker's ears perked up, and she wagged her tail again.

Maeve had never had someone to talk to while she baked. It was *really* nice.

The hours passed as she cooked, chatting to Baker, occasionally pausing to test something with a spoon.

Just before sunset, they took a break, and Maeve let Baker out into the yard to do her business again. She held the door, but kept her distance as best she could. Baker was a good dog, Maeve had to give her that — she came inside when called and didn't chase Macavity the cat, who had positioned himself on the fence, flicking his tail every so often.

After Baker was tucked back into the laundry room, Maeve fixed herself a quick dinner — a baked potato and rotisserie chicken. Baker gave her a look, and she shredded some of the chicken for her, placed it in a saucer and slid it across the floor.

The dog waited until Maeve was back in the kitchen before starting to eat.

That was fine. If they kept our distance from each other like this, she could handle taking care of a dog. Baker was surprisingly well-behaved. And mellow.

In a way, she was easier to hang out with than Emma.

She wasn't sure how she'd take it, but after dinner, she asked Baker, "What about some music?"

Baker, who'd already finished her chicken and lay back down on her blanket, wagged her tail.

Maeve found a happy playlist on her laptop, turned to her kitchen — which looked like a hurricane had hit it — and got back to baking.

Chapter Twelve

BAKER HAD NEVER SMELLED SO many amazing scents all at once. Maeve kept placing new pans on the black top of the counter. Soon after, steam would rise, and she would take a spoon and taste whatever was inside.

If it was too hot, she would yelp and dance around on the spot, then flash a smile at Baker.

Maeve was a nice lady.

It seemed like maybe she was nice all the time.

Was that possible? There hadn't been that many nice humans around before. Only Emma and Leslie. *Maybe* Dr. Dale. But they didn't ever touch her. Maeve petted her. And fed her chicken.

Baker's nose twitched at the memory and she licked her lips. That chicken had been tasty.

"Almost there," Maeve announced. "Will you help me, Baker?"

Her ears perked up. Every time Maeve spoke, Baker half-expected her to shout or throw something. But she never did. It was always something nice. Like the chicken. Or when she'd asked about the music coming from the radio on the counter.

It was boppy and thumped in her ears, like a tail striking

against a wooden pole, and a man howled over the beat. Baker liked it.

Maeve danced along to the music and turned in a circle. She came around the kitchen island, shaking her tail, or the spot where her tail should have been, and spun toward her. She put the spoon to her mouth and crooned a song, then pointed the utensil at her.

Baker stiffened and scrambled backward, but the spoon didn't fly free of her hand.

She held it, firmly.

Maeve blinked and stopped dancing.

"Sorry, I didn't mean to scare you." She paused and lowered the spoon. "I guess we're both scared of each other."

Maeve walked back to the other side of the counter and continued cooking, but she didn't dance as much anymore. She kept glancing sideways at the dog.

Baker laid back down on the blanket with a sigh.

The smells grew more intense, and Maeve flew back into action, opening cupboards and slamming doors, humming and sometimes dancing again. None of the other humans Baker had known had done this type of thing. They sat in front of the TV. A lot.

They'd never kept her inside either, not on a comfy blanket. They had tied her up outside or left her in the garden.

"All right," Maeve said, and dumped dishes into a big silver hole in the counter. She poured water from the faucet onto some of them, and steam rose from it. She opened the window and waved the steam out.

"Whoops!" She giggled. "All right, I think we're ready, Baker. Here goes nothing."

Maeve returned to the counter and brought out three plates. She dished up three different things onto them, balanced them on her hands and arms, and walked through the kitchen toward Baker. She placed them on the floor in front of the door, then backed up a few steps.

"There. Please don't try eating any of them. Just a sniff to test them and see if they're good. Oh, wait, I have an idea. Hold on."

Maeve rushed back through the kitchen and opened the big silver box in the corner. She took out a container, opened it, then brought it back.

"See?" She lifted out a piece of meat. "It's chicken. If you sniff and tell me which of these is good, you can have the chicken. Good idea?"

Maeve backed up and waited next to the kitchen counter, the box clasped between her hands. She sighed. "Please? Help me? Oh my gosh, I'm silly. I'm talking to a dog." She shook her head, hair falling around her face. "But I can't figure out if any of them are any good. It's like I've permanently confused my taste buds. Or maybe everything I'm making really is bad." Her lips turned down at the corners.

Baker got up from her blanket and pattered over to the plates.

Maeve perked up, nodding enthusiastically.

This was like the peanut butter cookie thing at the shelter. Emma had let her sniff the good and the bad ones, then gave her treats once she was done.

Baker lowered her nose to the first plate. It had a bowl on top with gloopy stuff inside. She sniffed it, but it smelled so cloyingly sweet, she sneezed. The gloop erupted from the bowl and splattered onto the floor. She tucked her tail between her legs, waiting for Maeve to shout.

"Well, I think it's safe to say that's not the one I'll be making." She laughed, came forward slowly, and lifted that plate out of the way. "What about the brownie?"

She sniffed the square of dark stuff on the next plate. Not overly sweet, like the first dish, but there was a strong bitter scent — and something faintly metallic that she didn't like underneath the good scents. She turned her face away.

"Okay, so I was right about that too. They taste okay, but

they're nothing special. They'd be a lot better with walnuts, but there's also nut allergies to consider. Another reason I'm not making those peanut butter cookies again." Maeve removed the square on the plate. "Okay, what about this one?"

She drew in a breath of the round cake with the streaking circles at its center, and wagged her tail. It smelled like flowers and fruit, and it reminded her of running through a field with the sun on her back.

"Really? You like it?" Maeve bit her bottom lip. "Perfect, I'll make the roly-poly cake. Our job isn't over yet, Baker." She removed the cake plate, then put the container with the chicken down.

It was all ripped up and shredded already, but Baker couldn't fit her nose into it.

"Oh, sorry." Maeve picked it up again, glanced over at her bowl. She shifted from one foot to the other, and the sharp tang of fear wafted off her again.

She was afraid. What had Baker done to warrant that?

She trotted back to her blanket and sat down, so the human could see she wasn't going to do anything scary.

"Thanks," Maeve said softly, coming in. She poured the chicken into the bowl, checked the water bowl, then hurried out of the room. She switched off the light, then shut the laundry room's funny half-door. "There. Safe and sound. Thanks for your help, Baker. Sheesh, it's stupid of me to be talking to you, but I guess … maybe I am going crazy."

Baker wagged her tail twice.

"Goodnight, Baker." Maeve walked off, footsteps echoing through the hall. A moment later, the kitchen light switched off.

Baker waited until it was silent, then she gobbled the chicken down. It was so much better than the food she'd been given at the shelter, although she'd been grateful for that.

She lapped up water from the bowl, then went to lie down

on her blankets again. For the first time in quite a while, she was comfortable and warm. Maeve's house was better than the shelter, no other dogs whining or snuffling. No cold cement floors. No cage. She shut her eyes and took a deep breath.

The soft pitter-patter of paws sounded outside her room, and she cracked her eyelids open.

A scratching came on the door. It creaked open a crack, and Macavity — that was what Maeve had called the cat this afternoon — poked his head around the door. His eyes glowed yellow in the thin beam of moonlight coming through the window. He stared.

Baker growled, but the cat didn't hiss or try to pee on anything this time. Instead, he wandered back out of the room and disappeared.

That was the way of cats — confusing.

But he had opened the little door that separated Baker from the rest of the house. Maeve hadn't clicked the lock into place.

Now nothing was stopping her from exploring the house.

But would Maeve get mad if she found her somewhere else?

She'd better stay here.

Baker tried shutting her eyes, but a soft yelp forced them open again.

What was that?

She got up and nudged the door open with her nose so she could poke her head out, lifting her ears to listen.

There it was again, coming from the living room. Like a hurt puppy, crying for help.

Baker left her blanket room behind and walked down the hall, stopping every few steps to listen. The closer she got, the more she wanted to whine at the sound.

She stopped in the living room doorway.

It was Maeve.

She lay on the sofa, lights off except for the flat black TV on the wall. It flashed white-blue pictures, quietly.

Maeve had her hand thrown over her eyes, and her chest shook. Every now and again, she would swallow. Her lips parted.

"Please, God, please help me get through this. Help me get what I want so I can … I don't know, eat? Live my dream? Please, please, let me make the right decisions. I've done so many stupid things lately. With David and with the cookies and now, with my clients. Please."

She broke into the quiet yelps again.

How many times had Baker yelped like that?

She stepped forward, claws clicking on the wooden boards.

Maeve stopped talking and lifted her arm off her face a little. She looked over and met Baker's eyes. She didn't shout or chase her off, but the sharp scent of her fear made Baker sad.

Baker was doing everything she could to show Maeve she wasn't going to hurt her.

Kind of like Leslie and Emma had done for her.

And even Maeve had been so careful not to do anything to scare her, it was getting easier and easier to believe she was really nice.

How could Baker convince Maeve that she was nice, too?

She walked to the sofa's side, turned in a circle and lay next to it, hind legs spread out nearest her head. She sighed, a big huffing breath.

Maeve shifted on the couch. Her hand came down and rested on Baker's back. She stroked her fingers through the fur.

Baker tensed and waited, but nothing else happened. She petted her, fingers massaging away the fear.

Soon, Maeve stopped yelping, and they both fell asleep.

Chapter Thirteen

LAST NIGHT, Maeve had decided that the roly-poly cake with raspberry preserves was officially the way to go. Today's mission was to figure out how to make it the most delicious roly-poly cake ever baked. With vegan ingredients.

She grabbed the grocery bags from the trunk of her car and carried them into the house, depositing them on the kitchen counter. Yesterday's experiments had used most of her vegan ingredients, so she'd gone back to stock up on everything.

This was how life was meant to be lived. On the edge. That, or she was slightly hopped up on natural fruit sugars and vegan-approved sweeteners from all the sampled raspberries. She sighed, grabbed a fresh shirt from the bottom drawer, and put it on.

Then she rubbed her palms together.

Baker sat in the doorway of the laundry room.

Maeve had a vague memory of lying on the couch, petting her while she sobbed all over her throw pillow about how she kept messing her life up. She remembered her fingertips touching warm fur, and crying harder, but also somehow feeling better.

But when she woke up this morning, there was no dog, and she wondered if she'd dreamed that.

Baker whined softly and looked down the hallway toward the back door.

Maeve let her out, barely shivering as Baker walked past her into Mom's garden. All day yesterday, she'd kept her distance, wagging her tail when she talked to her, sniffing whatever she put in front of her, and lying peacefully on her blanket the rest of the time.

She hadn't bared her teeth once. Or done anything even vaguely threatening.

Maeve thought maybe Baker was also being careful.

Baker came back inside, then returned to the laundry room doorway and sat, waiting patiently for food.

Maeve had bought dog food, too. And some of those biscuits Emma had given Baker when she first met her.

"Breakfast time," she said, and Baker backed up to the far corner of the laundry room so Maeve could fill her bowl.

She unpacked the rest of the groceries while the dog ate, and made herself a cup of coffee to go with one of the vegan brownies she'd made yesterday.

Not a bad breakfast, but for some reason, it had a faint metallic aftertaste that she hadn't noticed when the brownie was warm.

She tossed the rest of the batch and made a note, so she could compare with the results of her other experiments. If she could figure out which ingredient — or combination of ingredients — was causing that, she could avoid it in the roly-poly cake.

Or maybe she could let Baker smell everything and pick whatever the dog liked.

Maeve turned to find the dog staring from the laundry room doorway.

"Ready to do some more baking, Baker?"

She wagged her tail.

"Good. Then let's get started. The raspberry jam isn't quite right and the cake is a bit dry. I think that's because we can't use eggs, and the flax mix isn't—"

The doorbell rang.

Maeve went the long way around, through the living room so she wouldn't have to walk past Baker, and unlocked the front door.

Leslie Durant, the owner of Pretty Paws, stood on Maeve's doorstep, her face shining with a smile. The entire room lit up whenever she smiled, and the rest of the world with it. Maeve couldn't help feeling that Leslie had a good soul.

But that didn't explain why she was standing on her porch.

"Good morning," she said, and held out a cup of takeout coffee.

Maeve accepted it, even though she'd just drunk half a cup of her own. "I didn't expect company this morning."

"Is that your way of asking what I'm doing here?" Her dark eyes sparkled. She took a sip of coffee from her own take-away cup. "I don't mean to bother you, I just wanted to have a chat about Baker."

"Oh, of course." Maeve stepped back to let her in, and shut the door behind her. "I didn't mean to be rude. I'm just — sorry. Please excuse the kitchen; I'm getting things ready for a big baking project."

She was doubly glad she'd cleaned up after last night.

Leslie clicked her tongue. "You know I don't care about that. It smells amazing in here."

They walked to the kitchen, and Maeve set down the gifted coffee. "Thanks for this. I need all the caffeine I can get."

"Ready for the contest?"

"Nowhere near it, but I will be. I think I've chosen my dessert."

Leslie spotted Baker sitting in the doorway, and smiled at her. "There she is."

Baker barked and wagged her tail at Leslie.

Then Leslie turned back to Maeve. "I feel bad that Emma forced her on you. I know you're definitely not a dog person, and Baker's ... wow."

"What?"

"She looks better," she said, moving closer to the dog and peering at her. "Like she's stopped biting at the fur on her legs. The skin is less irritated than usual."

Leslie reached out in slow motion, to let Baker smell her hand.

The dog gave her a sniff, then licked the back of her knuckles.

"Is this even the same animal?" Leslie asked.

"Unless aliens snuck in last night and replaced her." Maeve forced a chuckle. "Baker's been helping me sniff out the best dessert for my contest entry."

"Incredible." Leslie looked almost dazed, but then she shook her head. "Listen, I wanted to offer to take her off your hands, if she's too much. Emma really shouldn't have done that to you."

"Oh." Maeve licked her lips, glanced at Baker, whose ears had started to droop. That shouldn't have bothered her, but it did. "But, I mean, Emma said you're really crowded."

"Well, yes, but I don't want you to feel obligated to anything..." Leslie let her voice fade, and something came into her expression that Maeve didn't know and wasn't sure she was meant to recognize anyway. "Would you like to keep her a while?"

No. Surely not. She'd only taken her in because Emma had implied that refusing was a death sentence for Baker, and she couldn't stand the thought that the poor dog might be put to sleep.

Except, it had been nice to talk to her while she was baking.

And she hadn't tried to bite. Hadn't even growled when Maeve got too close by accident.

And the brownie. She'd noticed that the brownie smelled off, even though Maeve had thought it tasted fine right after it came out of the oven.

And there was that maybe-dream that she'd come to the couch while Maeve was crying and let her pet her until she felt better.

When she thought about how quiet the house would be if Leslie took her…

"Baker's been really helpful, actually. With my … baking stuff."

It sounded like a lame reason, even to her own ears.

"I see," Leslie said, a small smile playing around the corners of her lips. "Why don't you keep her for another week? Give that skin on her legs a chance to heal up."

"Yes, totally! I wouldn't want her legs to get worse."

"That's a relief. We've just had another dog come in who could use her space. A real cutie, I'm sure we'll find an owner for her in a few days."

"Yeah, of course, no problem. I've got the dog food and stuff anyway, might as well use it up."

Leslie took another sip of her coffee, and the gesture was almost pointed, like it meant something more.

"Dogs are sensitive souls. They form bonds with the humans who take them in and care for them."

"What do you mean?" Maeve asked, glancing at Baker. Her ears flicked, and she tilted her head to one side as if she could understand what Leslie was saying.

"We have the best shelter in the area, and possibly one of the best vets in the state, but even he couldn't get Baker to stop chewing on herself, or to willingly leave her cage. Yet you've got her sitting calmly, right there in the doorway, sniffing your baked goods to help you win a contest. What do you think that means?"

"That dogs like things that smell good?"

"Think bigger," Leslie suggested. "What do you think it means in the grand scheme of things?"

"What are you saying?" Maeve asked, not exactly ready to buy soul bonds between humans and dogs just yet. Or at all. Baker was sweet, but she was a dog, and Maeve was still herself. "That this is fate or something?"

"I'm saying you two are meant to spend time with each other. I've seen just about every type of dog come through my shelter. I've watched owners find the mutts that make their life complete. There's always something special that happens when a person finds their dog."

"I don't know——"

"I specialize in rehabilitating psychologically-damaged dogs. I couldn't make progress with Baker in months, but one night with you and she's significantly better. What does that tell you?"

"That I give her loads of shredded chicken when she helps me out?"

Leslie chuckled, and Baker barked a second time, wagging her tail again.

"You can pretend you don't see it, but I can tell you feel that connection with her," she said, at last. "Poor Baker's been through a lot."

"Like?" Maeve drew closer, lowering her voice, as if she shouldn't talk about it in front of Baker, as if it would upset her. *Don't be ridiculous. She can't understand, not really.*

Still, she wouldn't have liked it if two people stood around talking about her and David, or the fact that she'd totally failed at opening a bakery of her own for the past five years, or how she'd lost a lot of work because of her obsession with the oven.

Leslie bit her bottom lip, then gestured through the doorway. "Let's talk in the living room. It's rude to chat like this in front of her."

So, clearly, Maeve wasn't the only crazy one who wanted to spare Baker's feelings.

Leslie chose Mom's favorite overstuffed chair. Maeve plunked herself on the couch, and had a brief ghostly sensation of fur against her fingertips.

That was a dream, she told herself. *If Baker had really appeared next to the couch in the middle of the night, you would've freaked out.*

"Baker's been through a lot," Leslie said. "More than most of the animals I've seen come through the shelter. She's been beaten, starved, left out in the cold, abandoned on multiple occasions. That poor dog has had more bad owners than good."

"That explains it."

"What?"

"How jumpy she is sometimes. Not that I'm one to talk. I was bitten by a dog when I was young. I had to get stitches on my cheek. See? You can sort of see the scar when I turn like this." Maeve tilted my head. "So I'm jumpy, too."

"Seems to me like you and Baker have a lot you could work through together. You're sure you don't mind keeping her a little while longer? No pressure. I can take her back anytime you'd like."

Maeve hesitated, teeth gnawing at her bottom lip. Yesterday, she would've jumped at the chance to let Leslie take Baker away. But now, the sad-melty feeling around her heart started up the second she imagined the dog leaving.

If she did keep Baker, what would that mean for the future? Maeve wasn't about to suddenly transform into a dog person, no matter how sweet that dog was.

Was she?

"Just for a little while longer," she said, at last. "Until her legs heal."

Chapter Fourteen

MAEVE'S GARDEN wasn't big, but there were lots of new smells out here, from the blooming flowers at the end of the garden, to the creeping vines along the back fence and the bugs that flitted about inside them. The dirt smelled so good, Baker got excited and started digging a hole in the corner, even though she didn't have anything to bury there yet.

Then she wondered if Maeve was going to get mad that she'd ruined her grass?

But Maeve just sat on the back porch, sipping on a drink, occasionally smiling or tilting her head back so the sun shone on her face.

"Isn't it a lovely day?" she asked. "Nice to have a break. We've been working so hard."

Baker barked and carried on digging up the dirt.

Maeve kept her distance. That was good, but sometimes Baker wished she'd pet her.

She buried her nose in the dirt and snuffled it. There was a smell below, something strange and damp. She chewed on the dirt and scratched some more. What was it? Something tasty.

"Oh, hello Macavity," Maeve said.

The cat sat on the fence, glaring. Baker lifted her snout and barked at him, shaking her rear-end this way and that, leaping and pawing the ground. *Do you want to play?*

Macavity turned away, lifting his tail into the air. *Play with this, peasant.*

Annoying creature. But that was fine. Baker could handle a cat, as long as he didn't do anything stupid, like peeing on the fence or attacking Maeve.

Then she would have to chase him up a tree. Which would be great fun, but she wasn't sure how Maeve would feel about it.

Baker scraped her paws through the dirt, but she couldn't find the source of that thick, moist smell. Finally, she gave up and trotted back to the steps.

Maeve stiffened for a moment, then relaxed and smiled. "Look at you. If you keep making a mess, I'm going to have to give you a bath."

She shook herself, splattering the porch with dirt. A glob of it landed in Maeve's cup.

She gasped and stared into it.

Baker tensed. The shouting would start. There was a stick nearby. What if she—?

But Maeve burst out laughing. "Now, you need a bath, and I need a shower."

Baker didn't like baths. The water was always too hot or too cold, and the soap stung when it got in her eyes. And when she struggled, people would tie her up so she couldn't run.

But maybe it would be different with Maeve.

"All right, I bought some stuff to wash you with. Be right back."

Baker wandered around the garden, sniffing at things while Maeve was gone. Macavity planted his furry butt on the top of one of the fence posts.

I'm the king of this castle, he meowed.

She barked back. *A king who steals chicken and tries to spray things.*

Macavity turned his head away.

Why don't you come down here and say that to my face?

He didn't respond, but lifted a paw and set about cleaning his claws. Somehow, he didn't lose his balance and fall off the fence, because of course he wouldn't. Baker couldn't run through the yard without tripping over something — of course the cat would be impeccably balanced and graceful.

"It's cleaning time!" Maeve called, as she dashed out of the back door and onto the porch, holding a large metal tub. She grinned and nearly tripped over the bottom step. "Whoops!"

She dumped the tub on the grass and lifted a bottle of red liquid out of it. Then she fetched a hose, nearly tripping over that, too.

Once the tub was filled, she turned the water off and said, "Can you please get in the basin?"

Baker snorted. Maybe a bath wasn't such a good idea.

"It's nice and cool. And it's such a hot day." She bent and dipped her hands into the water, flicked several droplets at Baker.

She tensed, but the water landed on her back and sank through her fur, nice and cool.

"See?" Maeve dropped a few on herself too, sprinkling them over her face. She laughed and patted her legs. "Come on. Come here, girl."

Baker bounded over to her, and Maeve helped her into the basin.

Then she took a deep breath and mumbled to herself. "It's okay, Maeve, you've got this. She's not going to hurt you. She's not going to—"

Baker wasn't going to bite, not ever. She licked at Maeve's palm to prove it.

Maeve patted her, gently, and they both relaxed.

"All right," the human said, taking a deep breath. "Now, for the shampoo."

She squirted a blob of floral jelly from the red bottle onto Baker's back. As Maeve scrubbed it in, it foamed all over her, even between her ears. She lifted a paw and plopped it back into the water, splashing some of it out.

It splattered everywhere, and Maeve laughed. "Come on, Baker, we're supposed to be washing you, not me."

Her laugh sounded like sunshine felt. Or like fresh-baked cookies smelled.

Baker couldn't stop wagging her tail. A bit of foam floated and landed on her nose. She sneezed, then shook herself off. White bubbles sprayed all over Maeve's dress.

She laughed and splashed flicked more water at Baker's side. Baker slapped the water with her paws and splashed back.

Maeve shrieked, but it was a happy sound. A yip of joy.

They splashed each other until the human's hair hung in wet strings around her face and the grass around the tub was covered in little clumps of bubbles.

"Truce!" Maeve said, still laughing as she got up to turn the hose on. "Let me get the rest of the soap off."

As soon as she finished rinsing her off, Baker hopped out of the tub and hurried over to the fence to shake herself off. She landed a few drops of water on Macavity, who gave her an indignant hiss and jumped away into his garden.

"You're such a troublemaker," Maeve called, approaching with a towel.

Nope. No towel. Baker was too pleased with her wet fur to let it go right now. She bolted away, kicking up clods of dirt, her tongue lolling out of the side of her mouth while Maeve chased her, out of breath but still managing to call and laugh.

Finally, she ran up the steps and sat on the deck.

"Oh, now you're done?" Maeve asked.

She toweled Baker off, and after she was dry, Maeve rubbed her ears.

Baker was so happy, for a moment she almost forget to be careful.

She could almost forget Michael kicking her, the old man who abandoned her in the park, the girl who left her for days without food.

Maeve wasn't like the others. She fed her chicken and noticed when she was scared and never forced her to do anything.

And her fingers were always gentle.

Baker wanted to stay with her.

Now she just needed to convince Maeve that she was worthy of keeping around.

Chapter Fifteen

"ALL RIGHT," Maeve said, grabbing the leash that Emma had left for her. "Are you ready to try going for a walk?"

Baker jumped off her blanket and wagged her tail.

The day had been a bit warm earlier, but now it was beautiful out, the late afternoon sunshine cooled just enough by a light breeze. The perfect opportunity to attempt walking a dog. If Baker would let her, and if she didn't lose her nerve before getting the leash on her collar.

Don't be silly. You washed her just an hour ago. This is nothing compared to putting her in a tub of water and scrubbing her.

That had gone surprisingly well. In fact, it had been fun, which was definitely *not* what Maeve had been expecting.

Who knew that dogs liked splash fights?

And the look on Macavity's face when Baker had run over to the fence to shake the water out of her fur — Maeve couldn't breathe, she'd been laughing so hard.

This should be way easier than that. Walking a dog was supposed to be fun.

Baker dropped her head a bit, like she was trying to make it easier to attach the leash. That was a good sign, right?

Maeve sucked in a breath, gathering whatever courage she

could find, and walked over to her slowly. She clipped the leash into the metal ring, then retreated to the laundry room doorway, just in case Baker decided she didn't like it after all. The plan, if she barked or lunged, was to drop the leash and shut the lower half of the door, keeping her there until she calmed down.

But all Baker did was look up, like she was waiting for a signal.

Phase One of Operation Dog Walk complete. Initiate Phase Two.

She led Baker to the front door, then grabbed her keys and phone before heading out. Baker stayed behind her at first, but as they turned right down the street, she pulled alongside and kept pace.

Folks strode up and down the street, some of them walking their own dogs or cats. Baker would veer away from the other animals when they came close, shrinking closer to Maeve's leg. Probably remembering the dog in the shelter that Leslie had mentioned her fighting with.

She had a hard time imagining Baker picking a fight with another dog. Even with Macavity, she only teased. And she'd been so playful during her bath.

Taking care of a dog was supposed to be a lot like taking care of a baby: messy, intense, and a lot of work.

But Baker had been no work at all, other than the work of staying out of her way.

In fact, she'd been excellent company.

Better than most people, honestly.

Maeve thought again about that dream of her lying next to the couch while she cried and pet her until she fell asleep.

At the time, she'd told herself it was a dream. Even if Baker could tell she was sad, she'd been afraid of Maeve — how ridiculous was it to think that she'd been trying to make her feel better?

But now she was wondering how true that might be. Baker seemed happy now, trotting beside her, veering off occasionally to smell the roots of a tree or to cock her head and watch a squirrel shimmy up its trunk.

The chirp of birds, the occasional chatter from someone's front garden, or tires passing over the asphalt — it all felt so wonderfully normal. More so than anything had felt since she'd discovered that David was cheating on her.

Her throat clogged up and tears stung the corners of her eyes, but this time, it wasn't because she was dreading what might happen next. It was because, for the first time since David, she felt like things could get better.

What if this could be her new life?

If she could win the contest, open her bakery, and spend the rest of her days inventing new pastries with Baker at her side?

If time off could be about quiet mornings drinking coffee while Baker played in Mom's garden, and splash fights, and walks?

If she could say goodbye forever to the Leroys and the Davids, and spend time with the people who really mattered, the Emmas and the Leslies and the Bakers?

Maeve was afraid to want that, because if she couldn't have it, her heart might break all over again.

And it was going to hurt ten times more than losing David ever had.

How could her life look so different now that Baker was here?

All she'd done was lie on a blanket and occasionally sniff stuff and wag her tail.

No, that wasn't true.

She'd also noticed that Maeve was upset and tried to help. Even though she'd been abused by humans her whole life, Baker had still detected her sadness and tried to comfort her, a human she barely knew.

This sweet dog wasn't just better company than most people. She was a better *person* than most people.

Baker slowed to sniff a leaf — or maybe it was the dirt underneath it? — and Maeve stopped, tucking her hand into her pocket and looking up at the sky. Sunshine warmed her cheeks, made her feel like she might actually be glowing.

It was hard sometimes to remember what happy felt like, but she thought this might be it.

Baker barked once and shifted, planting her feet in front of Maeve's.

Maeve blinked, shading her eyes to see who was coming toward them.

Jassie St. Claire.

It was like a movie villain had swung down from a skyscraper, weapon at the ready.

Except, Jassie's only weapon was her barbed tongue. She waved and called out, "Maeve, did you give up already?"

So much for remembering what happy felt like.

Maeve pretended not to hear. Maybe she could just walk past and Jassie would decide it wasn't worth the trouble today. "Let's go, Baker."

The dog looked up dubiously, but held her ground.

Jassie stopped in front of them, carrying a huge glittery purple purse. The purse shifted, then the top flap popped open and a tiny dog poked its fluffy head out. It barked, exposing ever-so-slightly-crooked but remarkably-white teeth.

"Sorry about that, Angelina Jolie doesn't like mutts," Jassie said, nodding to Baker.

Goosebumps prickled across her skin. "Excuse me?"

"Mutts. Mixed breeds. That's what your dog is, right?"

Baker wasn't her dog, but that wasn't the point.

"Let me guess," Jassie continued, checking her nails while her dog trembled and blinked its rheumy eyes. "You got it from that no-hope shelter at the center? I mean, that's really sweet that you take in charity cases and all. I guess it's the only place that lets *anyone* take a dog. Right?"

Baker looked up at Maeve again, like she was trying to

figure out why they were talking to this person. Then she sat down, one of her shoulders brushing Maeve's calf. She didn't growl or bark, but her furry eyebrows shifted as she studied the mini-dog in the purse. Maybe she couldn't figure out what it was, either.

"Is there a reason you stopped to talk to me?" Maeve asked.

"You're in my way," Jassie said.

She resisted the urge to point out that no one owned the sidewalk, and started to brush past her.

Jassie shifted sideways, blocking her path.

Here we go again.

"I hear you lost your job."

Her stomach curdled. "I'm freelance, so I can't lose my job."

"That's great, because I heard from one of Daddy's friends who works at HealthNut that your audition entry wasn't up to par."

"Weird, because they accepted me," Maeve replied, plastering on her brightest smile. "Daddy's friend must've been mistaken."

Baker shifted closer and leaned against Maeve's leg. Strangely, it made her feel braver rather than freaking her out. Like the dog was backing her up.

Who exactly did Jassie think she was, anyway? The Queen Bee of baking?

"They accepted *you?* What did you enter?"

"A simple peanut butter cookie. I figured it would be crazy to make something over-the-top, like, say, I don't know, a two-tier chocolate cake with live flowers on top."

Jassie's jaw dropped. When she'd tossed insults in the past, Maeve had never really pushed back.

It felt good to stand her ground for once.

"Clearly, making a cake like that would be too much for

some people." Jassie shrugged and touched her fingers to the top of the dog-rat's head. "But that's all right. You do you."

Maeve just shrugged.

"Great attitude," she continued. "It's just a baking contest, no big deal. Once it's over, everything will go on like normal."

That was below the belt. Everyone in Logan's Creek — including Jassie — knew that opening a bakery was her life's dream. And by now, they probably also knew that she'd been turned down for a loan by every bank in town.

"You won't believe what I'm entering, but it's a winner. If you need any help choosing something appropriate for your skill level—"

"I know what I'm making."

"I did mention that one of Daddy's friends is a major shareholder with HealthNut, didn't I? If you wanted me to run your thing by her and make sure it's not going to be too basic…"

Like Maeve would ever tell Jassie her plan. The last time she'd told her nemesis anything like that was senior prom. In a weak moment in Home Ec, she'd described the gown she planned to make for herself, her own design.

Jassie went home and persuaded her father to hire a French designer to come up with a dress that made Maeve's look like a cheap knockoff of hers, even though Maeve had spent six weeks working on it.

"You'll find out along with everyone else," Maeve replied.

"Oh come on, it's not like you have the talent to win or any—"

Baker barked at Jassie, drowning out the last part of her sentence.

"Wow. Control your mutt."

"Baker, what's wrong?"

But Baker took a step forward and barked again, glaring fiercely at Jassie. She didn't growl, and her hackles didn't rise.

It was a dead stare, right at the wannabe baker with the crimson lipstick.

"Seriously, this is what you get for adopting instead of buying a pedigree animal like my Ang—"

Baker barked twice in rapid succession, which set Jassie's pedigree rat into a flurry of yipping. Jassie clamped her lips together, tossed her hair, then marched off down the street in a cloud of indignation and designer perfume.

"What was that about?" Maeve whispered down at Baker.

Baker wagged her tail in response, and the expression in her eyes was practically a smirk.

The warm melty feeling was back. Had she just barked at Jassie to get rid of her?

"In that case, thank you." Maeve patted her head, and Baker wagged her tail so hard that her entire butt wiggled as well.

Somebody was getting a treat, as soon as they got home.

Chapter Sixteen

THE TWO THINGS on the plates looked the same, but Maeve wanted Baker to pick the one that smelled better. She had a tub of chicken ready, as a thank you for helping.

"Help me pick the winner. Which one smells better?"

Baker sniffed the first, licked her lips. It smelled yummy. Really, everything Maeve baked now smelled delicious. She sniffed the second one, but it smelled a little too sour. She poked her nose against the rim of the first plate and pushed it forward.

"Yes! Perfect. Okay, great. So, roly-poly number one is the success so far." Maeve picked up the plates and set them on the counter, then poured the chicken into Baker's food bowl in the laundry room.

"Good job, Baker!" She patted her head.

Baker barked, but this time Maeve didn't jump or give off that sharp fear scent. She smiled instead.

"We've done a lot of good work today. I think we should take a break. What do you say? Do you want to watch a movie with me? We could watch *Lassie*? That's a classic. I'll make popcorn. And, oh, I got these!" Maeve hurried back to the kitchen and produced a bag of crunchy treats. "You can have some while we watch. What do you say?"

Baker barked and wagged her tail, then headed for her bowl. Before she had any treats or watched a movie, she wanted to finish off the chicken, in case Macavity came by later to steal it.

As if summoned by just the thought, a trilling meow came from the door to the laundry room.

"Macavity. What on earth are you doing here?"

The cat wound away from the door and toward the kitchen table. He rubbed himself up against it, lifting his front paws and landing again.

"Do you want some chicken, too?"

That wasn't fair. Macavity hadn't done anything to help. Baker barked disapprovingly.

"No, you're right, Baker. Chicken is for the dog-sniffer." Maeve winked. "But I do have some tuna somewhere around here."

Macavity gave another meow and blinked slowly, big yellow eyes almost glowing in the dimness. *See? She loves me, too.*

This house isn't big enough for the both of us. A grumble rose from Baker's throat.

"What's wrong, Baker?" Maeve asked, her forehead crinkling with worry. "Do you hear something?"

Oh, no — she was getting scared again. Baker glared at the cat, trying to make it clear it was Macavity's fault for the noises coming from her throat.

Macavity wandered over to Baker and rubbed against her chest. Trying to make peace for the sake of the tuna. *What do you say, chum?*

I'm not your chum. Another grumble, as soft as she could make it this time. *I could chase you out right now.*

"Macavity, are you coming?" Maeve called, bringing out a tin and a can opener and popping the can, letting out a terrible fish scent.

Fine. But no peeing. Baker licked Macavity's ear, a show of good faith.

The cat purred for a moment, then darted off between the table legs to meow and rub against Maeve's legs.

Baker wouldn't chase the cat around the house because she didn't want to worry Maeve. She seemed to like him, though why anyone could like a cat, Baker would surely never understand. Who could like a creature that smelled like their own saliva and flicked their tail when they were angry?

Hadn't cats gotten the memo? Tail wagging was for showing joy.

It was no use worrying about it now. Macavity had his fish. Baker had her chicken. And Maeve whistled as she moved around the kitchen, smiling down at them every now and again.

Everything was good again.

"Only a few more days until the competition, Baker. I think, with your help, I'll make the most delicious roly-poly in the world, vegan or otherwise." She busied herself with pouring water into the basin, then started clanking and clinking dirty dishes in the water.

She did this often. And she sang along to music from her laptop and shook her bottom whenever she did.

Once Maeve had finished cleaning up all the dishes, Baker followed her into the living room.

"Okay," the human said, fiddling with the TV on the wall, and another thing sitting on a shelf beneath it. "I only have this because my no-good ex-boyfriend left it here, but whatever."

Baker settled herself in front of the sofa, sitting upright, just as Maeve said, "Shoot, I almost forgot the treats."

She rushed out again, passing Macavity, who leapt onto an armchair and promptly proceeded to lick himself in the most indecent places.

He looked up, eyes wide, as if he could feel Baker's attention on him. *What?*

Baker turned away. A truce didn't make them friends.

Maeve was back in no time, carrying the bag of doggy treats and a bowl of salty, buttery popcorn.

She gave Baker a treat, then ate a handful of fluffy white popcorn, making a lot of crunching sounds.

"I never watched this with David. He wanted me to, but I said no dogs, no matter what." She smiled. "But maybe he left it here for a reason."

Baker thumped her tail against the sofa. No, it wasn't bad at all. Even with Macavity massaging a cushion on the armchair and purring too loudly.

Maeve grabbed a piece of black plastic with very chewable buttons from the coffee table and pointed it at the TV.

"Ready, Baker?"

Baker licked her knee, tentatively.

Maeve giggled. "That tickles!"

Then the TV did that thing where it turned into a window. But a really weird window — when they looked through it, it didn't show the backyard like it should.

Baker ran to the other window, to make sure Maeve's garden was still there. It was.

Then she ran back to the couch to look at the weird window, which looked out onto a house that definitely wasn't in Maeve's garden. A boy and two adults stood in the yard, talking.

"It's not a window," Maeve said, laughing. She did something with the buttons and the people froze. "This is the movie."

Macavity glared down from the armchair. *Stupid dog.*

Baker sat next to Maeve and licked her knee again.

Now she got it, this was what TVs did. Through it they watched a sad boy meet a really smart collie — they became friends, and the collie saved the boy from a wolf. But then the boy thought the collie had died and he was so sad, Baker couldn't help whining when he cried.

Maeve reached out to pat her on the head. "It's okay, Lassie isn't really dead."

And she was right, because Lassie came back to surprise the boy.

Baker was so happy, she jumped up and barked and ran in a circle.

Maeve laughed. A lot.

Macavity went back to licking himself.

After Maeve had finished her popcorn, she lay back on the sofa and dropped her hand onto Baker's back.

Lassie had protected the sad boy from a wolf, just like she'd protected Maeve from the mean girl with her teeny dog. She'd found a home by making the boy happy again.

Maybe that was all Baker had to do: make Maeve happy. Then she'd be allowed to stay.

Chapter Seventeen

Was she really doing this?

Maeve had spent a lot of time thinking about it last night after the movie — lying on the couch after laughing so hard her stomach hurt — she hadn't laughed like that in a long time.

Not since before her mother died.

She thought she was happy with David, but he never once made her laugh like that.

At the time, she'd blamed it on the Leroys, and on her love-hate relationship with running her own graphic design business.

She'd loved design when she started playing around with online tutorials in high school, but as soon as she needed to do it for a living so she could stay home and take care of Mom, she'd grown to hate it.

Mom had made her promise that after she passed, Maeve would quit freelancing and start her own bakery.

But after the funeral, Maeve had been in a daze, too numb to do anything but tackle new orders as they came in. That daze lasted until she met David — but he always said it was crazy to walk away from a thriving business that brought in enough to pay for expensive vacations and all the other things they did together. Normal couple things.

Honestly, Maeve had wanted to lose herself in what felt like a normal life. Normal had left her forever the moment Mom got her diagnosis.

But last night she realized that she didn't want normal.

She wanted happy.

And last night, she'd actually felt happy. Thanks to Baker.

How could Maeve take her back to the shelter, to live in a cage, waiting for someone to love her enough to adopt her?

Assuming that she would be adopted at all.

No, she couldn't risk it.

Baker deserved a real home, and Maeve wanted to give it to her.

"We're going on a trip," she said, clipping Baker's leash onto her collar.

The dog wagged her tail so hard, she accidentally whacked it against the wall. But if it hurt, that didn't stop Baker from looking up, eager, as Maeve grabbed her tote and led her outside.

Even though they'd never gone anywhere in the car together before, Baker jumped onto the back seat and lay down. Strapping her in was a little tricky, but she held still as Maeve fumbled the seatbelt around her.

At one point, their faces were next to each other's, and a flicker of old fear stoked in Maeve's belly.

Then Baker licked her chin.

This was absolutely the right thing to do.

But was she really ready to be a dog owner? What if it all went wrong?

Maybe she was making a bigger deal out of this than it was, but it felt huge. Like a life decision.

Maeve didn't have a great track record when it came to making life decisions.

Baker barked, and Maeve glanced at her in the rearview

mirror. She sat straight, pressing her nose to the back window, smudging it. She wagged her tail. For the entire ride, Maeve could hear the swish-swish-swish as it swept back and forth across the vinyl seat.

"We're almost there." They pulled into a parking space in front of the shelter and got out.

But as soon as Baker was out of the car, she lifted her nose to the air, sniffing hard.

Then her entire body seemed to droop, as she understood where she was again.

Maeve grabbed the leash. "Come on, girl. I promise, you're going to like what happens next."

But as she took a step toward Pretty Paws, Baker planted her butt on the ground, looking up with those big, brown puppy dog eyes. She whined.

"Don't worry, Baker," Maeve said, and stroked her head and ears. They were silky soft. "After today, you'll never have to see this place again."

That got Baker walking again, reluctantly.

Maeve led her through the front door. Her tail was low and tucked between her legs, obviously unhappy.

Maybe she should've come in to make it all official without Baker, but she hadn't wanted to leave the dog a long in the hot car.

Funny that it only crossed Maeve's mind now that she maybe could've left Baker at the house. But she'd never even considered that option.

The receptionist — a redheaded woman, not the pink-haired teen from before — smiled at me. "Hi there. Can I help you?"

"Hi, yeah, I'm here to—"

"Oh hey, Maeve!" Emma called from the passageway leading to a door in back. "You brought Baker? What are you guys doing here?" Emma was clearly in the middle of dog-washing duties. She held the leash of a big black dog who'd been brushed until its coat appeared glossy. Rottweiler, I guessed.

"Yeah, I just came to—"

The Rottweiler barked loudly, baring its teeth.

Baker barked back.

Emma said something, scolding the big black dog. It lunged forward, and Emma's feet slipped out from underneath her.

She fell backward, throwing her hands up. The black dog streaked into the lobby.

Maeve screamed and dropped the leash, backing away, but the Rottweiler wasn't interested in her. It dove for Baker.

Both dogs erupted into a flurry of barks and bites, lunging and dodging, sometimes rising onto their hind legs. Teeth flashed, and the round whites of their eyes showed. Growling and snapping filled the lobby, louder than the elevator music coming through the tinny speakers. Baker yelped as the dog bit down on her back.

"Hey! Leave her alone," Maeve yelled, forcing herself forward. "Emma!"

Emma was already on her feet, rushing toward the dogs, as was the lady at the reception desk.

Maeve grabbed hold of Baker's leash again and pulled on it, trying to drag her away from the black dog. "Stop. Please, stop!"

Blood trickled from the torn flesh on her back as she shook and strained against the leash, trying to get at the other dog.

Maeve shook, too, with adrenaline and fear and fury at the black dog.

Baker hadn't been doing anything, and he attacked her. She'd only been defending herself.

Emma grabbed the other dog by the hips and dragged it back an inch or two. Both dogs still snarled at each other, saliva flying, their hackles raised.

"Baker." Maeve touched her back, trying to comfort her.

She spun around, growling, teeth bared.

Then she bit Maeve's leg.

Maeve screamed as pain shot through her calf. Icy panic raced through her veins, and her vision tunneled until all she could see was Baker.

She dropped the leash and scrambled backward, up onto the nearest chair.

The redhead took the Rottweiler by the collar, physically dragging him through the door back to the cages.

That door slammed shut and Baker shrank back into a crouch. Her fur fell flat against her back again and she tucked her tail between her legs. She pressed herself to the floor and crawled toward Maeve, whining.

"Get away," Maeve shrieked, the pain in her leg growing sharper by the second. She looked down, but saw no blood seeping through the denim. Not yet.

"Maeve, you're okay, it's over," Emma said.

"She bit me!"

"She was scared. She panicked."

"SHE BIT ME!" Maeve knew she was repeating myself, but she was panicked, too. She'd trusted Baker, who'd seemed sweet-tempered until now.

She'd trusted Emma, who'd promised me that her fear of being bitten again was unfounded.

She'd trusted Leslie, who wanted her to believe that she had some sort of special connection with an animal who couldn't control herself.

Baker's been on good behavior all week, but this is who she is.

And Maeve been about to adopt her.

Baker whined and wagged her tail, creeping closer and closer.

Maeve would've scooted farther backward, but the chair she'd hopped onto was already pressed against the wall.

"Maeve, just breathe." Emma held out a hand, maybe to

help Maeve dismount from her precarious perch, or perhaps just for comfort. "Why did you bring Baker in, anyway?"

Because I'm an idiot who thought a dog could be my friend.

"Never mind," Maeve said.

And bolted.

Chapter Eighteen

Bully ruined everything.

Baker hadn't meant it. She'd been scared and forgot Maeve was behind her.

When she'd felt the touch on her back, Baker ahd thought she was another dog, sneaking up from behind.

She didn't mean to bite her.

She tried to say she was sorry, that it was an accident.

Maeve left anyway.

Baker was alone again.

She went to the door that Maeve had run through and scratched at it, but she didn't come back.

She stood up and looked out through the glass and whined, but the door didn't open.

"Oh Baker, I'm sorry." Emma's eyes were watery with tears.

"He's back in his kennel," a woman said from behind, the one who took Bully away.

"I can't believe I let him get away from me." Emma wiped her cheek with the back of her hand.

"He's a problem. I've been saying it for a month now. Can't trust him with other dogs."

"There are no problem dogs. Only problem people who caused the behavior." Emma picked up the abandoned end of Baker's lead. "Come on, Baker, honey, let's go. I don't think she's coming back."

No more shredded chicken. No more sniffing Maeve's creations. No more movies or digging in the garden or splashing in the tub.

Baker had never had any of that before Maeve. And now she would never have it again.

Her insides felt hollow. She'd been abandoned by humans before, but she'd never missed any of them before.

She missed Maeve.

"This way, girl," Emma said, sniffling a little. She tugged gently on the leash in the direction of the kennels.

Baker sat down, whining.

Maeve had to come back. She didn't want to stay here anymore. It wasn't home, and she didn't belong.

She kept whining and pulled on the lead. Maeve needed help with her baking.

She doesn't want you anymore. You bit her.

It was a mistake. She hadn't wanted to hurt Maeve. She loved her.

But Emma shook her head and opened the door to the kennels. "Come on, I know this sucks, but…"

The other dogs barked as she dragged Baker into the kennel, and all of their barks sounded like jeering.

What is she doing here?

Ha! Her new owner didn't want her.

You missed playing with me, didn't you?

The last bark was from Bully, who was settled back in his kennel.

Baker ignored him especially.

"I'll get Dr. Dale," Emma said.

But even though her back stung where Bully had sunk his teeth in, that was the least of the pain.

Dogs barked and pressed their noses against the bars of their cages as Baker passed.

The cacophony hurt. Baker hung her head, her nose overwhelmed by the smell — urine and kibble and disinfectant.

Emma stopped in front of the only empty kennel and swung the door open. The blankets were in there, neat and clean.

"It's not so bad," Emma said, but she hiccupped and pressed her fist to her nose. "In you go, Baker. Just for now. I'm going to try and figure this out."

Baker whined once more and dragged herself inside, then lay down on the blanket. There was nothing wrong with it, but the blanket didn't smell like roses and vanilla, like the one at Maeve's house.

Emma closed the door and secured the latch with a metallic click.

"What's going on?" Leslie's voice rang out. "What's Baker doing here? Oh, honey, what's wrong?"

"Maeve left her," Emma said.

"What? The last time I saw them together—"

When Emma explained what happened, Leslie's lips drew into a thin line.

"This is all my fault. If I'd just grabbed Dom in time, Maeve would have adopted Baker."

"Adopted her?"

"I think that's what she was coming here to do," Emma said. "Finalize the adoption. But now it's all ruined. Poor Baker."

Each time she heard Maeve's name, Baker's insides got hollower. It wasn't hungry pain — she was plenty familiar with that — but a deeper one that wouldn't go away. It didn't matter how she shifted position or how she breathed. It stayed.

"I'm going to call Maeve and find out if she's okay," Emma said.

"You do that. I'll get Dr. Dale." The women walked off together, their voices fading.

Then it was quiet except for the odd bark or whine. The brown-nosed dog across from her wagged its tail. *Hello.*

Baker didn't wag back.

She closed her eyes. Maeve had proven that loving her was impossible.

For the rest of her life, Baker would always be the dog that nobody wanted.

Chapter Nineteen

MAEVE STOOD IN THE KITCHEN, heart *ka-thumping* in her chest, and pressed her palms to the counter on either side of her miniature roly-poly. The contest deadline was just days away, but she was no longer sure that what she'd chosen as her signature product dish would work.

She'd made dozens of versions, but without Baker's sensitive nose, she couldn't tell which was best.

Her calf throbbed as she remembered the fight between Baker and that other dog, the flash of teeth as Baker had turned on her when Maeve tried to calm her. The pain was all memory — Baker's teeth had only grazed her skin, leaving pink marks that faded soon after she left the shelter.

Left Baker. Even though she was clearly hurt.

Left her in a place where that big black dog could bite her again.

She bit you.

But maybe Maeve was the one who'd betrayed her.

She'd burst into tears as soon as she made it to her car, then cried all the way home.

Harder than she'd cried when Jassie stole the boy she knew Maeve had a crush on.

Harder than she'd cried when she found out David was cheating on her.

The only time in her life that she'd ever cried that hard was the night Mom died.

That was the last time she'd felt like her life was over.

How could she be this broken up over a dog she'd known for barely a week?

A dog who attacked her — out of panic, yes, and after she'd been attacked herself — and okay, maybe Maeve should've known better than to touch her before she felt safe.

Somehow she'd come to trust Baker, and she'd just assumed the dog trusted her back.

She took a breath.

She'd thought she was ready to adopt Baker, but clearly she wasn't. She didn't know the first thing about handling a dog, especially one that had been traumatized. The first time something went wrong, all the trust Maeve thought they'd built evaporated, and Baker reacted like Maeve was a stranger trying to hurt her.

Her calf throbbed again in phantom pain, sharper than before.

But the bite wasn't the worst hurt. Much worse was the thought of Baker being afraid of her.

The dog might even have realized what she was doing and stopped herself — she could have sunk her teeth in deep, torn a chunk out of Maeve's leg.

Instead, she barely left a mark. A warning nip. *Don't touch me right now, I'm freaking out.*

Baker might have been trying, but she'd also been seriously damaged by her previous owners. Leslie was the best animal psychologist in the state, and even she couldn't help her.

Why had Maeve thought that she could?

Baker would've bitten her sooner or later, it was only a matter of time. Better that it happened sooner, and that she went back to the shelter so she could find someone who knew how to help her.

And Maeve … she had a baking competition to win.

By herself.

Without anyone to stop her from second-guessing every little change she made to the recipe.

She was in so much trouble.

What would Mom tell her to do?

Take a deep breath and get clear on what she needed to do — the essentials, not the million things she *could* do.

She grabbed her laptop from the living room, brought it back to the kitchen, and opened the email from her assigned HealthNut representative, received earlier this morning. She scanned it, her heart sitting in her throat.

Dear Maeve,

My name is Jeffery, and I'll be helping you get acquainted with what's expected from you for the HealthNut contest. As one of only 200 other contestants, you will have the opportunity to prove that your product is the one to enter the HealthNut rotation.

Should you win, you will receive a cash prize and your name credited on our websites as one of our creators. I'm sure you're very excited to hear more about the opportunity, and what you need to do to have the best chance of winning.

So, here's what you'll need to do:

- *Show up by 8am on the day of the contest. There will be several rounds during which live judges will test your product.*
- *Be prepared to bake on site. Bring your ingredients in clearly-labeled containers. You will be expected to finish your product within a one-hour window. You will be allowed to pre-bake components if your recipe takes more time to prepare. However, be aware that this will affect your final score — production time is a crucial factor for judging.*

- *Wear your contestant entry number on your shirt. You will receive the number at sign-in the morning of.*
- *Be prepared to answer questions from a panel of journalists and media representatives. The contest winner must be capable of representing HealthNut in public appearances and media interviews.*
- *There will be three elimination rounds. The winner will be selected at the end of all three rounds.*

Please feel free to email me if you have any follow-up questions. Good luck, and may the best baker win!

Maeve's stomach squirmed like it was full of worms. This was her last chance. If she blew it, she was doomed to a life of kissing up to Leroys.

Focus, Maeve.

She'd already timed herself with the roly-poly cakes and making the preserves to fill them. With Baker's help, she'd found the perfect balance of sweet and tart that brought out an intense raspberry flavor. The sponge cake took between forty-five minutes and an hour, because it had to cool before it could be rolled around the jam, so she'd be cutting it close.

Maybe she could bring a small battery-operated fan to cool it faster? Then she'd have time to not only roll it up, but give it a dusting of freeze-dried raspberry powder and shredded coconut.

You can do this.

But the doubt was there.

At the beginning of this week, she'd been so sure that the roly-poly mini-cakes were the winner. Baker had liked them the most. Experimenting with the vegan ingredients had been the real time-suck — if she could use butter and sugar and cake flour, she'd have been completely confident. But now it seemed impossible that she'd figure out which of a million variations would taste the best. Every time she tried the new batch, she couldn't help comparing it to what her grandmother's roly-polies tasted like, and of course they came out wanting.

She was almost ready to throw it all away and start again with a different type of dessert.

"No, you can't do that," she said, aloud to herself to make herself believe it. "There isn't time to start over."

Maeve glanced up at the laundry room door. She didn't have the heart to remove Baker's blanket yet. It sat in the corner, near her water bowl and empty food bowl.

Her eyes prickled with tears.

"Don't be ridiculous. Everyone's better off now."

Baker had been hurt so many times in the past, and Maeve wasn't qualified to look after a dog that needed special attention like that. She would probably have wound up damaging her more somehow, without meaning to.

Leslie wouldn't give up on Baker. She would find her an owner who could make her happy. One who was really meant to look after dogs with psychological trauma, and who wasn't so scared of them.

So why couldn't she stop missing the sweet little dog?

The whole Baker thing would pass. Maeve would get over it, just like she'd gotten over David and the fact that he was now traveling the world with a model.

Yeah, keep telling yourself that.

She shoved the negative thoughts aside, double-checked that her apron was tied firmly in place, and began measuring ingredients for the next batch of roly-poly cakes.

By the time the raspberry mixture started to simmer, she'd lost herself in the process. Everything was fine until she asked, "Nothing but rice syrup for the batter this time, or half rice syrup and half coconut nectar? What do you think, Baker?"

She looked up at the empty spot in the corner of the kitchen where Baker liked to sit while Maeve baked.

She stopped stirring and swallowed. Again her eyes grew

hot, and her stomach sank. Because again, she'd forgotten the dog was gone.

Maeve turned her back on the laundry room for a moment and tried to catch her breath. This was silly. She'd lived without Baker for her whole life. She didn't need a dog.

What did she even miss anyway?

Baker spent most of her time lying on a blanket, watching Maeve cook.

She couldn't talk.

She couldn't bake with her.

All she could do was listen.

And make her laugh.

And stand up to Jassie.

"Just stop," Maeve mumbled, and got back to work on the cake.

She timed herself prepping the cake and came in at just over an hour. Not good enough.

If the judges knew it took that long for her to finish the bake, then surely that would dock her score. Time was money, after all.

Maeve grabbed a dessert fork from the top drawer, wishing Baker was here to give it the old sniff test, then cut off a piece. She shoved it into her mouth and chewed.

The raspberry preserves didn't have that perfect sweet-sour tang they'd had in the last batch. The cake was soft, but not light as air. Maybe it was a mistake to add a bit of chickpea flour to the batter?

Maeve groaned and dumped her fork on the counter. "What now?"

She had to keep trying, even if that meant baking all day and all night.

Alone.

Before she met Baker, that had been her definition of heaven.

But now, it felt like hell.

Chapter Twenty

BAKER HUDDLED at the back of her cage and wondered what Maeve was doing now. Baking, probably.

Or maybe watching a movie with Macavity. Petting the top of his head. Letting him sniff whatever she'd just made and asking him what he thought.

Maeve would never come back. Baker had bitten her. She wouldn't let her apologize, to try and make up for it, because like most humans, she hadn't cared. Not really.

But Baker still missed her.

Sometimes, after the lights went out in the shelters, the other dogs would whine or howl. Especially the ones that were new. Baker joined them. Her chest was hollow, even when her belly was full.

The dog in the kennel directly across the hall from her was barely more than a puppy, with big eyes and floppy ears and a tail that wagged for everyone. He sat with one paw on the door of his cage, head tilted toward her as if asking what she was doing there.

Because humans are mean, she wanted to explain. They'll lock you up without any food or leave you outside in a storm or kick you when you're doing your best to make them happy.

And sooner or later, they get tired of you and leave you somewhere to take care of yourself.

But she didn't want to scare the poor pup, and what was the point? He'd find out soon enough for himself what humans are like.

Unless he got adopted by someone like Maeve.

And if that was going to happen, she really didn't want to scare him. Because if he accidentally panicked and nipped at his owner, it would be Baker's fault when his human brought him back here.

Or took him to one of the bad shelters.

So she flicked her tail at him, a little moment of connection and encouragement across the empty hallway.

He lifted his ears at the sound of the kennel room door opening and closing. The other dogs jumped up and started barking, begging for Leslie's attention as she came down the hall looking them over.

She paused at Baker's kennel, her fingers running softly over the links of the kennel door. Baker flicked her tail, reaching for something that struggled to approach pleasant, but she knew Leslie wasn't fooled.

Leslie wasn't the sort of human who was easily fooled.

But she turned away from Baker's kennel with little more than that short glance and crouched down in front of the puppy's kennel. The pup hopped and barked, pleased to have Leslie's attention.

"What about it, Brownie?" Leslie asked. "Let's go to The Front and meet the nice lady."

She brought Brownie out. He jumped up to lick her face and hands while she attached the lead to his collar.

Like many dogs who went to The Front, Brownie didn't come back. By the end of the day, there was a new dog in his cage.

When the lights clicked off that night, Baker thought of Maeve and howled like a motherless pup.

Chapter Twenty-One

One day until the contest, and Maeve was not ready.

She scuttled around the kitchen, cleaning up after another batch of roly-polies gone belly-up. There had been something wrong with every batch she made.

One batch took too long to make.

Another batch had a texture that was less Victoria sponge and more kitchen sponge.

Yet another batch had scorched a little because she'd turned the temperature up to see if she could shave five minutes off the cooking time.

The latest batch had that metallic taste Maeve thought she'd gotten rid of when she'd eliminated quinoa from the flour mixture, and she wasn't sure if she was imagining it or if she'd screwed up the flour mixture again.

She *needed* a second opinion.

She opened the fridge and peered inside, then grumbled to herself. "Out of raspberries again."

The only positive of being totally occupied by the baking contest was that she hadn't had time to panic over the mounting stack of bills on her entrance hall table. And BestGig still hadn't reinstated her account or even replied to her help request with more than an autoreply: "We appreciate your patience as we investigate this complaint."

If Maeve didn't win this contest, she was going to have to rebuild her client list from scratch.

"Focus," she muttered, as her gaze slipped toward the laundry room door again. It was ridiculous, but she still hadn't moved any of Baker's things. She didn't have the heart to. It was as if she expected to open the door and find her waiting there.

"The raspberries." She stripped off her apron, checked her hair in the reflection on the oven door, then hurried outside, grabbing her purse and keys on the way.

She got into her car and tried to start it. The engine didn't turn over the first two times she turned the key, and she fought down the urge to scream. Not the car, too!

Was everything in her life going to fall apart?

On the third try, the engine sputtered to life, and Maeve reversed out of the driveway. Macavity lay on the fence, watching with cool yellow eyes.

He hadn't come into the house since Baker left. Was he angry?

Now she was worrying that the neighbor's cat might be mad at her?

This baking contest had melted her brain.

The drive to the grocery store was okay, until she passed the road she would've turned down if she were headed to Pretty Paws.

Then she wondered how Baker was doing.

That Rottweiler had bit her, really bit her, actually hurt her. The thought of her huddled in her cage, her torn flesh bleeding into matted fur, made Maeve's heart ache.

But the shelter people would make sure the wound was cared for. If it got infected, Dr. Dale would give her antibiotics.

Maeve, on the other hand, couldn't do a single thing to help her. Baker was better off without her.

What if someone else had adopted her?

Leslie wouldn't give her to just anyone. She'd make sure that whoever took Baker home had the skill to handle an abused animal.

Emma would tell her if Baker had been adopted, wouldn't she?

Or try to. Maeve had about thirty voicemails and twice that many texts from Emma that she'd been ignoring, because she was still mad that her friend had convinced her to trust Baker.

As soon as she pulled into the grocery store parking lot, Maeve checked her texts. The latest messages were all apologetic pleas to call her.

Maeve listened to the latest three voicemails. Same thing. No mention of Baker being adopted. Or dying of gangrene. Or being killed in another fight with the Rottweiler.

She's fine, stop worrying.

Maeve pushed open the glass front door and waved to Hank behind the front counter. He waved back, but continued talking to the woman in front of him, swapping stories about whatever gossip had taken the top rung on the ladder.

It was none of her business. She had baking to do.

Maeve grabbed a basket from the floor and set off down the aisles, swinging it as merrily as she could, even though she didn't hold any joy in her heart.

She looped into the produce aisle, hoping there were still raspberries left. She'd bought so many from Hank's in the last week, it was a miracle he'd been able to keep them stocked. Good thing they were in season. Frozen wouldn't cut it.

She stopped and picked up an apple, pressing it to her nose, inhaling its fruity scent. She reached for a smile, but it didn't come.

"Maeve? Is that you?" The familiar voice sent a chill down her spine.

Please. Not now. Anything but this.

"Maeve!"

She turned and saw her ex, David, striding toward her. His arm was around his girlfriend's shoulders. She wore a string bikini beneath a sheer sarong dress. What was this, Bali? They were in central Ohio, nowhere near any coast.

"It is you," David said, grinning like an idiot.

He was as handsome as ever, but with more of a tan, probably thanks to his Hawaiian getaway. He ran his fingers through dark, tousled hair, heightening the effect of casual yet attractive dishevelment.

Strangely, seeing David didn't bring on a rush of regret and sadness. He was the idiot who had ruined it all, and Maeve was … what? Willing to give up when the going got rough? At least, when it came to Baker.

Enough about the dog!

"How long has it been?" David asked.

How long had it been since he'd cheated on her? With the woman standing next to him?

"I'm sorry," Maeve said. "I'm kind of in the middle of something."

"Right, yeah. But this is crazy. I come back to town after my vacation, and the first place we go … just wow. Isn't the universe beautiful?"

Trying to screw Maeve over, more like.

He introduced Beach Babe, whose name was shockingly old-fashioned. Clara.

She flashed a set of perfect white teeth and extended her hand. "It's so nice to meet you. I've heard so much about you."

Maeve shook it — even her fingers were pretty, thin and soft, with perfect French tips.

"David talks about me?" she asked, tempted to counter

that she hadn't heard anything about her until she'd actually found out he'd been cheating on her. But cattiness would just make this even worse than it already was. Maeve was not going to have a meltdown in the fruit aisle of Hank's store, to be the main character in whatever story he'd be telling the next customer after she left.

Clara bit the corner of her lip and twirled one braid around her finger. "David told me all about how he helped you grow."

Helped her grow a sense of disenfranchisement and a deep distrust of men, sure.

"What am I, a houseplant?"

Clara giggled, as if Maeve had told the funniest joke.

"No, no," David said. "I just, like, firmly believe that life is all about growing, you know? We were each other's spiritual teachers, learning from one another at the soul level."

Maeve frowned. "If that's what we're calling it."

"What would you call it?" David tilted his head as though genuinely curious.

"I guess what I'm saying is I hope you learned an important lesson from our relationship," she said, and looked pointedly at Clara. "Not to be unfaithful. People deserve better than betrayal from the person they love."

"Whoa, your energy is really dark." David waved a hand. "Have you tried natural healing? Or reiki? Clara's taught me all about it. Clear out those clogged chakras. You're full of—"

"I'm going to cut you off there. I've got important things to do."

"Like what?" Clara asked, blinking, her green eyes sparkling.

Was she totally unaware of how awkward this encounter was? Or was she playing dumb?

"My entry's due tomorrow for a baking contest. I've got to shop for ingredients."

"A baking contest. That's so cool!" Clara clapped her hands, rattling her many beaded bracelets.

"Don't get your hopes up, Maeve. Remember, the universe gives us what we truly need."

Where did he get off telling her not to get her hopes up? After all the muffins he gobbled up while they were together?

"I never thought that what you needed was to be, like, a baker," David continued. "You've always been more of a 'salt-of-the-earth' kinda person."

He stretched out an arm, like he wanted to take hold of her shoulder. Maeve stepped out of reach, leaving him clutching air. It didn't stop him from adding, "Do what you're good at instead."

She walked off before she could give in to the temptation to bang him over the head with her basket. What had she ever seen in him? He'd pulled the wool over her eyes for so long, she'd been blind to all his faults.

He hadn't been into all that woo-woo stuff when they were together, either. He'd fancied himself a gourmet with excellent taste in graphic art.

But apparently he was a chameleon, ready to be whoever his next conquest wanted him to be.

When they were together, he'd done what was best for him, but Maeve had never done what was best for her.

She circled the store's perimeter, waiting until they'd gone before returning to the fruit. She walked up and down the open fridges, searching for her raspberries. She finally reached the section and stopped. Her heart nearly stopped, too.

There were no raspberries. The section was entirely empty.

"Hank!" Maeve yelled and dropped her basket. "Hank?"

"Up front," he called back.

She rushed through the aisles, apologizing over her shoulder to Miss Greene as she nearly ran her over. She reached the counter and caught herself on it.

"Good heavens, Maeve, what's gotten into you?" Hank smoothed his combover down, like he was the one who'd sprinted through the store.

"Raspberries," Maeve managed, gasping in breaths. "Where are the raspberries?"

"Oh, right. Jassie came in and bought them all this morning."

"She what?"

"Bought them all. And my back stock. And the new stock that came in too. Said something about making jam the right way. I should have some more coming in this weekend, though. Nothing to worry about."

Maeve's stomach dove to her knees. She resisted the urge to grab Hank over the counter and shake him by his apron straps.

"Hank, the contest is tomorrow. I can't make my entry without raspberries."

"We got plenty of other fruit — a batch of summer apples, including some Red Astrachans — and lots of cherries and blue—"

"Raspberries, it has to be raspberries." She'd spent the last week getting the filling for the roly-poly cakes as close to perfect as she could. If she switched to another fruit, she'd never have time to get the proportions right, even with Baker's help.

And she wouldn't have Baker's help.

Her desperation must've shown on her face, because Hank said, "You might be able to drive to the next town over and get some?"

But that would take half the day. If she lost that much time to driving, she wouldn't be able to test out her baking and timings properly. She wouldn't be adequately prepared. She pressed her hand to her forehead, breathing hard.

Maeve should've expected Jassie to play dirty. She'd probably come in here and chatted Hank up, found out that Maeve had been buying raspberries in batches. It would be nothing for her nemesis to buy every raspberry Hank intended to carry until the contest deadline was past.

Jassie had won.

YOU'RE CRAZY. You should go straight home before someone sees you.

But the tension had finally reached its boiling point, and the lid of Maeve's proverbial pot was about to shoot off and splatter jam all over the place.

She stopped in front of the grand gates at the St. Clair mansion, scowling so hard her forehead hurt. She rolled down her window and hit the button for the intercom.

It buzzed, then clicked.

A flurry of yipping came through the speaker, then Jassie's voice. "Who's there?"

The camera swiveled on the gate overhead, turning toward her car. Great. Jassie could see her.

"What an ugly car." That last part was whispered, but loud enough for Maeve to hear. "Shush, Angelica, we mustn't be rude."

"I've come for my raspberries."

A pause. The camera turned again, whining on its track, and Maeve cleared her throat.

"What raspberries?" Jassie asked.

"The ones you bought from Hank. I want them back."

"No idea what you're talking about." She clicked off the line. The gates didn't open.

Maeve beat her fist against the steering wheel, strangling a scream. She knew this was pointless, but she couldn't help herself.

A woman walking a Yorkshire terrier peered in at her. She pursed her lips, and Maeve stopped beating her steering wheel.

"Crap," Maeve whispered. "No way. This isn't fair. She can't do this to me."

She hit the button again. Another buzz and a click. More yipping from the dog-rat.

"Yeah?"

"I'm not messing around. I don't know what your problem is, but you're going to give me those raspberries right now. Or I'll … I'll…" What could she do? Scream and bash the intercom box?

That would probably get her arrested.

"I have no problem with you. A wolf doesn't worry about the opinion of sheep. Goodbye." Click.

Maeve punched the buzzer with her index finger, actually hurting it a little.

Click. "Go. Away."

"I want my raspberries." She dragged her wallet out and waved it at the camera. "I'll pay you for them. Don't you want to compete properly? On even footing?"

Another pause. Click. "If you don't leave right now, I'm calling the cops. This is harassment."

If she couldn't afford to spend half the day buying raspberries in the next town over, she definitely couldn't afford to spend the night in jail, waiting for Emma to bail her out.

"Fine, be like that! It doesn't matter who wins tomorrow, because I'll have won the moral victory."

Maeve trembled with anger.

Don't let her get to you, she's not worth it. That's what Mom would've said.

But Mom wasn't here. And Jassie was getting to her.

No way was she letting her win, money or not.

Maeve would do whatever it took to beat her.

Chapter Twenty-Two

"We've got to do something," Leslie said, crouching in front of Baker's kennel. "She can't go on like this."

Dr. Dale was hunched over next to her. "How long has it been since she last ate?"

They consulted the clipboard hanging on the kennel door. "Two days. I don't know what to do with her, Dale." Leslie's eyes were filled with worry. She smelled strange, a sharp current of fear running under the usual soft doggy scent of her clothes and skin.

But it didn't matter. Baker wasn't hungry. She gnawed on her itchy hind leg, worrying the fur away from her skin until she tasted blood.

"She's worse than yesterday," Dr. Dale agreed

"I think she misses Maeve."

The mention of her name tugged at Baker's attention, but she knew Maeve wasn't coming, so there was no point in hoping. She had to keep reminding herself of that. She dug in deeper with her teeth, desperate to get at that impossible itch.

"Baker," Dr. Dale called, softly. "Honey, look at me."

She glanced up at him.

"There we go, all right." He opened the cage door and came inside.

Baker didn't growl, but she tensed. She didn't want to be touched.

But Dr. Dale's hands were soft. He lifted her head, gently, just under the chin, and shone a light into her eyes. Then he touched the itchy leg. "We'll keep an eye on this. Might have to put a cone on her if she doesn't stop."

Leslie sighed.

"Has she been getting much exercise?"

"No, she won't go out into the yard, even alone, not without a lead, and she's so resistant to that I don't wanna force it too much."

Dr. Dale rubbed Baker's head once, then backed out of the kennel and shut the door.

Baker sighed and closed her eyes. She was so tired, but she couldn't sleep. She used to dream about running through golden fields, or chasing mice. Not anymore. When she did dream now, she was alone in the dark, sometimes in the rain or thunder.

"Was there anything that might've happened with Maeve? Did you see anything?" Dr. Dale's voice was gentle like his hands.

"Just a happy dog soliciting attention. She'd even stopped chewing at herself," Leslie said.

"She was eating there?"

"It looked like it." Leslie huffed out a breath. "I think she misses her. Baker finally found her home, and now she's back here."

Baker bit back a whine of misery.

That's exactly what had happened, and there was nothing she could do to change it.

She was all alone, and that's how it was going to be for the rest of her life.

Chapter Twenty-Three

MAEVE TORE INTO HER DRIVEWAY, still on the brink of tears. All the happiness she'd felt in the past week was gone, and a part of her couldn't shake the feeling that it was, in part, because Baker wasn't around.

When the dog had been here, things were more fun. Jassie had been a mere frustration, not a complete block.

Maeve didn't bang on the steering wheel again — if she broke a bone in her hand, she was out of the contest for good. She wanted to howl at the sky, but she held the noise in, just in case her next-door neighbor was feeling tetchy.

She closed her eyes and rested my forehead on the wheel of her beat-up Honda instead.

No matter what she did, she was doomed.

If she drove to the next town for the raspberries, she'd barely have time to bake three or four batches before she'd have to sleep.

Assuming she could get to a grocery store before they closed.

And assuming that there was a mom-and-pop store there that cared enough to source their berries from a local farm. Any berries she'd buy at a big chain would be shipped in a refrigerated truck from some mega-farm where they'd been harvested a week ago. Big chain berries were bred for shelf-life first and flavor second. They definitely wouldn't be organic, like the ones Hank bought from the grower's co-op just outside of town.

It was staring to get late, and each passing second heightened her panic.

The car's interior grew hot. She didn't have AC in this old thing, and rolling down the window would let in the sights and sounds from outside. Her failure would feel more real if she could hear the birds chirping, the distant drone of a lawnmower or the canned laughter from the neighbor's TV — he turned it up too loud because he hated wearing her hearing aid around the house.

The tears spilled over.

"This is your rock bottom. The freelance work has dried up, you're going to lose the competition, and Baker—" Maeve choked on her name.

What was wrong with her?

She hadn't wanted a dog in the first place. But now it felt like a little corner of her heart had gone missing.

All it had taken was a few tail wags. A chase around the garden in the sun. Laughing and splashing each other with soapy water.

She'd listened while Maeve talked and seemed to understand. She could still see her lying on that old blanket on the kitchen floor, one ear pricked upward while the other flopped.

Maeve had never understood before why dog owners were so crazy about their pets, but now, she got emotional just thinking about Baker.

Macavity jumped onto the hood of her car and planted his furry butt on it. He meowed loudly.

"What?" Maeve asked.

She half-expected him to dart off, but he just sat there, staring an accusation. Was he angry with her for taking Baker away? He hadn't come into the house, begging for food. Not since she'd left Baker at Pretty Paws.

"Macavity." Maeve tried to sound stern, but her voice wobbled after all that crying. "Come on, get off my hood."

He flicked his tail and didn't move.

"We couldn't keep her forever. The plan was always to give her back."

Apparently rock bottom included trying to explain her decisions to a cat.

Thankfully, her phone rang before she could embarrass herself further.

Emma. "Hey, Maeve, you feeling better?"

"If I say no, will you listen to my meltdown?"

"Your totally justified meltdown," she said. "Let me have it.

So Maeve told her — everything. Her failed attempts to perfect the roly-poly cakes. Seeing David in the store with Clara. Jassie buying all the raspberries, ruining Maeve's chances of winning.

"But that's not the worst," she confessed, crying again. "I can't stop thinking about Baker. I just abandoned her, and I'm all alone, and not even seeing David with his model girlfriend upsets me as much as that does."

Emma was quiet for a second on the other end of the line. "So, what are you saying?"

"I don't know. I'm scared that she'll turn on me, and that she might need an owner more experienced than me. But I miss her. A lot." Macavity thumped on the windshield with one paw. "Also, this cat from next door is staring me down right now, and I'm convinced that it's because he misses Baker. And if that doesn't make me totally loopy, then I don't know what does."

"Oh, there's no denying you're a total crackpot," Emma said, laughing. "But I think … Maeve, I think you should give it a real shot with Baker. She misses you."

"How do you know that?"

"Because she's sad." Emma's voice hitched. "I forced her on you the first time, and that wasn't right. Do what's right for you."

Maeve exhaled, slowly. The possibility was so tempting, but she had to be honest with herself. Was she ready to have a dog? It had seemed so easy while Baker was with her. But what if there was something she wasn't seeing? What if the dog was actually aggressive? No, that didn't sit right. Emma had explained in a bunch of her voicemails that the other dog had been picking on Baker for a while.

"As for the fruit debacle," Emma continued, "why does it have to be raspberries?"

Maeve started to explain about flavor profiles and perfect jams, but gave up a moment later. "There just won't be time to bake and test all the batches I'd need for getting it right."

"What if I was your taste tester?"

"Maybe. The cake is pretty good, so if I focused on the jam, and making it right for the version of the cake I've got now—"

"Blueberries," Em said. "I was shopping this morning before work, and Hank had loads of them. I'll pick up everything he has on my way over."

Her heart flooded with gratitude — Emma had just given her back her chance to win the competition. "You're the best, Em."

Macavity flicked his tail again. Then he jumped to the ground, disappearing into the neighbor's yard. Maeve sensed that the cat wasn't her friend anymore. At least, not until he got what he wanted.

For her to bring Baker home.

Emma had said she was sad. What did that mean? Had another dog attacked her again?

Maeve could make sure that Rottweiler never bit Baker again, but could she make sure Baker never bit her? They'd already had one incident — what if there was another one? Something worse, because no one would be there to pull her away.

Why couldn't anything be simple?

Maeve's hands tightened on the wheel. She could go over to the shelter right now and claim her. She still hadn't thrown out any of her things. She'd left Baker's room — when did she start thinking of the laundry room as Baker's? — exactly as it had been on the morning she'd lost her.

You're going to get out of this car, go inside, and start setting up to make another batch of roly-poly cakes. You're going to win this contest.

And if she did, maybe, just maybe, she'd have the guts to bring Baker home.

Chapter Twenty-Four

Maeve got out of her car, carrying her ingredients for the big bake-off, blood rushing in her ears. This was it. She had her apron on, her hair tied up tight, and her eye on the prize.

Well, for now, her eye was on the check-in desk.

The woman behind it smiled at her, took her name, then handed her a sheet of paper with the map of the area and a contestant number. There were stations for the contestants under a big white tent.

Maeve followed her map, clutching the wicker basket that held her ingredients to her side, ignoring the fluttering in the pit of her stomach. She had to find her station and get set up in time to be ready when they started the clock.

Then the tasting and the judging, and she'd know for sure.

She just had to keep it together until then.

The tent was a mess. Folks from all over had come for the competition and were setting up at their stations. Each one had an oven with stove top, a counter, and all the necessary equipment.

It was pretty awesome, and most of the contestants were in the process of setting up and chatting with their tablemates — they'd been grouped in twos.

This was it.

The flutter in Maeve's gut intensified. There was so much competition, and so many of the other contestants looked happy and confident. As she passed station after station, she gawked at others' ingredients. A lot of overlap with hers, but every time she saw something she hadn't tried, she couldn't help wondering if *that* was the secret that would've made her roly-poly cake a winner.

She found her station and placed her wicker basket on the counter so she could start unpacking her stuff.

"Oh, no way." The voice had come from behind her, bitter and sickeningly sweet.

Maeve turned around, and her excitement took a dive. Jassie.

She flicked her hair and placed the basket of her ingredients on the counter beside Maeve's.

"Is this a joke?" Maeve asked. "Because it's not a funny one."

"Don't think you can steal my idea." Passive-aggressive had flown out the window today, apparently. That had to mean Jassie was stressed about the competition — she wasn't even attempting to keep up appearances. "You've already lost."

A microphone squealed. One of five judges had risen from the table on the center dais —a gray-haired man, tanned, and energetic-looking, dolled up in a dark suit and bowtie.

"Welcome, everyone, to the HealthNut Baking Contest. My name is Arthur Jacobson, CEO of HealthNut, and I hope all of you are ready to compete. The first round will begin when the buzzer rings. You'll have to cook and complete your product in the allotted hour, no exceptions. When the hour is up, there will be two rounds of judging: a preliminary taste test to eliminate products, and a secondary round to find our winners. The third round of judging will determine which of the eliminated contestants produced the best product for a bonus fourth place prize."

Maeve's heart skipped a beat. There was more than just first prize, but those second, third and fourth places wouldn't net her enough money to open her bakery.

"Are you ready to go?" Arthur Jacobson beamed at them.

Jassie looked as if she'd just taken a face full of pie.

Maeve applauded and cheered along with everyone else.

The buzzer sounded, and she flew into action. She got the rest of her pre-measured ingredients out in a flash, set the oven to the correct temperature for the cake, and started with the jam.

She caught Jassie's eye only once, when she poured the blueberries into the pot. Jassie was clearly furious that Maeve managed to get around her little raspberry trick.

Ha. Nice try, Jassie.

Maeve forced herself to ignore her nemesis — to ignore everything — and just do the thing she loved most.

But even though she could shut Jassie out, she kept wanting to talk to Baker.

Kept imagining the dog lying next to the counter as she beat the batter.

Kept wondering if the version of vegan blueberry roly-poly cake that Emma had helped her create last night was the same version she would've arrived at if Baker had been the one to help.

A huge digital countdown had been erected next to the judge's table, and she kept her eye on it, her stomach quivering every time she looked up and saw that another minute had passed.

There were only ten minutes to go by the time her sponge cake was out of the oven, and four minutes when the battery-operated fan had cooled it enough to spread with the jam and roll into a log. Hands shaking, Maeve cut the log into neat slices, arranged them on the presentation plate, and garnished with shredded coconut.

The buzzer went off.

"All right, time's up!" Arthur Jacobson announced. "Great work, everyone. If you haven't managed to finish your product, I'm afraid you're eliminated. Please move to the spectator area on the far side of the tent."

A groan rose from several tables, and dozens of people start walking — about a quarter of the contestants hadn't managed to finish on time. Unfortunately, Jassie wasn't one of them.

Maeve peered at Jassie's counter out of sheer curiosity.

Her eyebrows lifted. *No way.*

She'd made cookies. Not a fancy double-tiered cake. Maeve opened her mouth, but decided better against asking — Jassie was too busy making eyes at the judges and smiling brightly to pay attention to Maeve anyway.

"All right," Arthur said. "Let the judging begin."

The judges came down in a group and walked among the tables, tasting each entry and marking off things on their clipboards. They worked their way through the hall clockwise. The closer they came to Maeve's counter, the more nervous she got.

She wiped my sweaty palms on her apron.

"Ew, try not to be totally gross," Jassie hissed.

"Leave me alone," Maeve snapped back.

The judges arrived at their counter, and they both lit their million-watt smiles.

"What do we have here?" Arthur asked.

"Well," Jassie said loudly, immediately drawing all the attention, as usual. "I made a completely healthy carob-chip cookie."

"That sounds interesting," Arthur said.

Seriously? She made a carob-chip cookie. Anyone can make one of those. That's boring!

Maeve couldn't help the internal monologue. It was just … she'd spent so long worrying about this roly-poly and working on it and now, this? She prayed the judges would share her opinion.

But they tasted one each and made appreciative noises as they ate. Not a good sign. Jassie grinned broadly. "I made extras in case you wanted to take some home," she said, drawing another sheet from the countertop to her left.

"We have to save space for the other contestants," Arthur said, and moved on to Maeve. "What have you baked for us, Contestant 987?"

"I'm Maeve, and I've made a blueberry jam roly-poly for you to try. Gluten-free, allergen-free, vegan, containing four superfoods."

She'd had to list the recipe on the form when she'd checked in, so they'd know whether her treat fit the nutritional profile they'd specified in the rules.

"Wow," said a female judge. "That's impressive."

"Thank you." Maeve fiddled with her apron.

They picked up their desert forks and each took one bite. The female judge seemed particularly enthusiastic. But more than she'd been for Jassie's dumb carob cookies? Maeve wasn't sure.

A camera crew followed behind the judges, and Jassie was already primping and preening for it, smiling and fluttering her eyelashes. Maeve did her best to smile and nod as the cameras and the judges moved on.

Afterward, she slumped.

It was over. The rest of the contest was officially out of her hands, and now Maeve could breathe.

"What are you so nervous for, Maeve?" Jassie asked softly. "It's not like you had a chance to win."

Maeve resisted the urge to snap back at her. The acceptance letter had been very clear that she would also need to have the demeanor HealthNut expected in someone representing them. Starting a cat fight before they'd even finished round two would disqualify her.

She could worry about getting last words in later, after the results had been announced.

It took the judges loads of time to make their way around the tent, and while they did, others entered: people taking seats in the spectator section, and family or friends who'd snuck in to offer encouragement to contestants.

No one would come for Maeve today. Emma was busy, and Maeve had pretty much isolated herself from everyone else after what happened with David. It had been difficult to show her face to her old friends after they heard everything about the breakup from other people first.

Still, that wasn't important. Maeve was here to win and start her life anew.

Finally, the judges returned to the main stage.

Arthur Jacobson took up the microphone and the chatter quieted.

"We've got our winner, our second place finalist, and our third place. After the announcement of the top three, we ask that you all remain in the hall for the awards ceremony, followed by the party for all participants.

Breathe. Just breathe. You've got this.

"The following contestants are in the top ten. Contestant 752."

Jassie erupted in a tirade of giggles and excited claps. She had made it through.

Arthur rattled off another six numbers, but none of them were Maeve's. Then another. And another one. There was only one spot left, and it wasn't her. It couldn't possibly be. Her roly-poly had failed after all. All her dreams—

"—Contestant 987."

"That's me!" Maeve yelled, and a few people laughed. "Oh my gosh, that's me."

Maeve had made it to the top ten. Her bakery was still in reach.

Jassie rolled her eyes. "Don't get your hopes up."

"Careful, the cameras are watching," she said, even though they were actually trained on Arthur and the other judges.

Jassie instantly straightened and put up her winning smile, twirling a length of curly brown hair around her finger. Then she realized no one was looking and broke into a scowl. "Funny."

Maeve ignored her.

"All right, time for the fun part," Arthur said. "In third place, with a frankly delicious mini tarte Tatin, is Contestant 366, Martin Krieg!"

A smattering of applause rang out, and a man on the other side of the hall cheered and whistled, then did a silly dance. Nearly everyone laughed.

"Very well done, Martin. We found it perfect, but perhaps a bit too complicated for our product line," Arthur said, then cleared his throat. "In second place, with a blueberry roly-poly cake, contestant number 987, Maeve Watts!"

Maeve's stomach dropped, but she forced herself to smile and clap along with the others. Second place. She had gotten second place. That was good, but it wasn't enough to start her bakery. Still, it was a cool ten grand she could use to pay off a big chunk of her debts. Maybe that would improve her credit score enough to somehow qualify for a loan? That cheered her up even more, and her cheeks felt suddenly warm. She waved and curtsied at the judges, which brought another round of applause from the crowd.

"And in first place, with the most delicious carob-based treat we've ever tasted, is Contestant 752, Jassie St. Clair. Congratulations."

Jassie shot Maeve a long, spiteful look and then threw her arms above her head and cheered.

How could this have happened? A carob cookie? Carob was an inferior substitute for chocolate — and chocolate was a superfood, so why hadn't she just used that?

Maeve Googled it surreptitiously. It looked like chocolate had something called oxalates in it, which could cause kidney stones, but carob didn't.

Jassie had done her homework. Or more likely, paid someone to do it for her.

Beaten by a carob cookie.

It had to be some kind of fluke.

Or maybe Jassie had beat her fair and square.

It was enough to make Maeve believe that David might be right. Maybe she should give up on baking and do what she was good at.

Right after she figured out what that was.

Maeve struggled to keep a pleasant expression as the reality sunk in. She lived in a world where Jassie St. Clair's carob cookies were deemed better than her blueberry roly-poly cakes.

"Thank you everyone for participating. As requested, please wait at your counters for the awards ceremony as we complete our final round of judging for fourth place. And congratulations to all of you — only a few of you could win, but we tasted so many amazing healthy treats today. You can all be proud of what you've accomplished."

Arthur Jacobson set down the microphone and was off to judge the final round.

"I win again," Jassie said, sneering. "I guess I *am* better than you."

Chapter Twenty-Five

MAEVE SET about cleaning up her station and packing the remains of her ingredients back into her wicker basket. She didn't have a sink to wash anything in, but from the looks of it, the other contestants were leaving their bowls, pans and utensils for someone else to take care of.

Not having to clean up for once was kind of nice.

"It was just such a simple thing to do," Jassie was saying, at her counter next to mine. The camera crew had swept in to interview her as the winner. "Carob is the perfect replacement for chocolate, and super healthy, too. My cookies are suitable for any diet — vegan, vegetarian, Paleo, keto — everyone can eat them."

Maeve forced herself to keep a straight face, but it was torture listening to her brag about winning with a concept that had been around since the 1970s.

"Maeve!" The cry came from the front opening of the tent.

Maeve rose on her tiptoes and craned her neck. Emma waved as she pushed her way through the crowd that milled around the tables.

"You came," Maeve cried, waving back at her. She hadn't

expected it.

"Uh, excuse me, the winner is, like, trying to do an interview," Jassie said, then turned back to the man with the microphone. "Sorry about that. She's just a runner-up."

Emma came closer, holding something low at her side, her brown eyes practically glowing with excitement. "Congratulations on second place."

Maeve shrugged, not trusting herself to say anything. Later, she would unwind with Em, and a good stiff drink or three, but for now, she wanted to be a good loser.

"Look who I brought," Emma added, and lifted her arm. She held a leash, and at the end of it was Baker.

Tears rushed to Maeve's eyes.

Baker looked positively forlorn. Her legs trembled, her ears hung low, and her gaze roved over the ground. The side of her leg had been chewed on, the fur there matted with some thick white ointment.

None of that mattered. It was her. Baker.

Maeve was taking her home.

"Did I do a good thing?" Emma asked.

Maeve nodded wordlessly, emotion building in her throat. She had been so afraid of this poor dog, and all Baker really needed was a bit of love. It had taken the misery of the past few days without her, and losing this contest, to realize that she mattered more than everything else.

"Baker," Maeve said, her voice cracking.

Baker's ears pricked up instantly, and she looked up toward Maeve. Her tail wagged weakly.

Maeve crouched down behind her counter and opened her arms. "Come here, girl."

Baker hesitated. She wagged her tail again.

"It's okay. Come here."

She darted forward at last, letting out a terrific bark that brought a scream from Jassie.

She launched herself into Maeve's arms, and for a brief

moment, the old panic resurged, but she caught Baker and hugged her tight. The dog wriggled happily, licking everything she could reach — the side of Maeve's neck, her cheek, her ear.

Maeve didn't even care that she was crying.

Baker pulled back, wagging her tail so hard that her entire back end wiggled, and licked Maeve's face. She froze, but Maeve didn't. She stroked her head.

Then she kissed her dog, right between the eyes.

"There. All better."

Baker barked again, and Maeve was sure it was agreement.

"Thank you. Thank you so much."

"I have to get back to the shelter," Emma said. "I'm not strictly supposed to be here. Want to keep Baker with you for a while?"

Maeve nodded so hard, it hurt her neck.

"Good. I'll stop by with the adoption papers later on."

With Baker snuggled up against her, nothing could bring her down. Not even losing to Jassie. Not even the possibility that she'd never own her own bakery.

This dog had shown her how to be happy, something she thought she'd never feel again after Mom died.

Maeve sat next to her counter and Baker crawled into her lap. She curled her arms around her and held her to her chest, stroking her head. They both let out a long, rough sigh.

"Dogs aren't allowed here," Jassie spoke above them. "It's a health code violation. Probably."

Maeve ignored her. Jassie hadn't broken her after winning the competition, and she certainly wouldn't now, not with Baker here.

"Do you see this? This is flagrant disregard for the rules," she said to one of the cameramen. "I'm just going to go get the judges right now and have her disqualified."

"There's nothing in the rules about pets, so far as I know."

He pulled back from the camera and frowned at Jassie. "What's the matter, lady? You don't like dogs?"

"I do like dogs." Jassie turned her frown upside down, really fast. "I love them, actually. I have two of my own, but I wouldn't bring them to a baking competition. It's just not the thing you do, you know? There are people eating around here."

"So? It's not like the dogs are doing the baking."

Jassie and the cameraman fell into a heated debate on whether animals should be allowed near food or whether Maeve should be disqualified. She didn't listen. Poor Baker felt lighter than she should. Maeve couldn't wait for this to be over so she could get her home and give her a big bowl of shredded chicken.

Plus, it would be fun to stand on that podium they'd set up on the dais with her, just to annoy Jassie even more.

The cameraman eventually gave up on Miss St. Clair's snooty self and walked off.

Jassie huffed and puffed. "You get that dog out of here, or I'll tell the judges."

Maeve finally shifted Baker off her lap and stood. "You got what you wanted. There's no need to be so mean about it."

Jassie set about piling the carob cookies onto a plate, likely to go butter up the judges even more, or maybe distribute them to VIPs. Like Daddy's friends.

"Whatever. I'm done spending time with losers." Maeve's nemesis dumped the last of her cookies onto the plate. "I've got a photo-op to attend to. Enjoy hanging out with your smelly dog."

At least my dog can't be mistaken for a rat, Maeve could've said, but didn't.

Because Jassie St. Clair was the least important person in her life.

Chapter Twenty-Six

BAKER LAY in the gap between the counters, wagging her tail at anyone who walked past. Maeve had forgiven her! She'd hugged her and kissed her and said she was happy to see her.

"Get out of the way," the mean woman named Jassie said to Maeve.

Something heavy collided with Baker's rear end, and pain streaked through her leg. She yelped and sprung to her feet.

A plate cracked on the ground in front of her and cookies spilled across the grass. They smelled good, but different from the ones Maeve had let her eat the first time they met, at the shelter.

Baker's stomach growled.

She hadn't eaten since Maeve had dropped her off at the shelter.

"Baker," Maeve called. "Are you okay?"

Baker leaped up and gobbled the cookies, swallowing as many of them as she could. They were bitter and sweet at the same time. Not nearly as good as Maeve's. But she was so hungry.

Jassie got up and stomped her foot. "No! Get off my cookies, you nasty dog."

"Eat whatever you like," Maeve muttered. "If you can stand the taste of carob."

"Is there a problem here?" A tall man approached. He was dressed all in black.

"Her stupid dog just ate all of my competition cookies," Jassie said. "I'm the prize winner. I insist you do something about this."

Baker finished the cookies and sat down, letting out a satisfied burp. Maeve stepped up beside her and put her hand on her head. "She's not hurting anyone. Jassie wasn't paying attention to where she was going and tripped over my dog."

The guy sighed, tugging on his ear.

"How did I wind up here?" he asked under his breath. "Get a job in security, honey. It will be fun. You'll make a lot of money this way. Thanks, Sharon, thanks for your lovely advice."

Baker tilted her head to one side, one ear flopping up, confused by the man's mumbling.

Maeve cleared her throat. "Excuse me, sir? Are you okay?"

The big guy dropped his hand from his face.

"I'm fine," he said stiffly. "But you two aren't. Keep it down in here."

"But what about the dog? It can't stay. Look at all the chaos it's caused. My dish is broken." Jassie bent and picked up the plate's pieces, which she shook at the man. "I'm the winner of this competition. You're supposed to do what I want."

"Look, lady, I don't care who you are. Or what the dog did. All I care about is that you behave yourself until it's time to go home. Or I'll kick both of you out."

"Well, this is just great," Jassie said after he left. "Now, I have nothing for my photo op." She dumped the pieces of plate on the counter above Baker's head.

Baker barked, and Maeve stroked her ears again. "Never mind her, Baker, she's not worth it."

"This is so typical of you, Maeve. You were always trying to make yourself look better than me."

"Huh?" Maeve shook her head. "Jassie, what are you—?"

"You could never stand it that people liked me, so you tried to be this goodie-goodie sweetheart that everyone loves. Now that I've finally beaten you at something, you have to try to sabotage me after the fact."

Maeve didn't smell like fear at all, just like her normal flowers and cookies and butter. "Don't act like you didn't enter this competition just to mess with me."

"How dare you!" Jassie put her fists on her hips and glared at Maeve.

A growl sat in Baker's throat, but she caught it between her teeth and held it, tight as prey in her jaw. She wasn't sure if Maeve wanted her to. But she didn't like Jassie. Jassie was mean to her human.

"How dare you accuse me of cheating?"

"I didn't, you said that," Maeve replied. "The point is, I didn't do anything to you, and I never have. I don't know why you have a problem with me, but it doesn't really matter right now. You got what you want, so leave us alone."

Jassie opened her mouth to argue, but a tapping noise interrupted her, and she turned away.

"Ladies and gentleman." A man stood on a wooden stage in the middle of the tables. "My apologies, but it will be a while longer before we can start our party. It appears one of the judges has taken ill. Please be patient and enjoy some refreshments while you wait."

The sound of retching from somewhere further back in the tent followed his words. He put down the microphone and hurried off somewhere.

"That's just great." Jassie threw up her hands. "If you think I'm sitting here with you and that smelly dog, think again." She marched off toward a man with a black box on his shoulder, who stood talking to more people.

"Good riddance," Maeve sighed, and patted Baker's head. "Do you mind staying here with me a while?"

She barked, her tongue lolling out the side of her mouth.

There was nowhere else she wanted to be.

Chapter Twenty-Seven

IT SEEMED there would be yet another delay before they could go home. Apparently, the onsite doctor had sent one of the judges to a hospital because of an obscure almond meal allergy.

Maeve had Baker to keep her company, and Jassie had been flirting with the cameraman for the past half hour. She would come over every now and again to say something mean, but it no longer bothered Maeve.

The disappointment of not having made it had yet to sink in. Or maybe, it was that she had still gotten second place. She'd have some money to get started; it would just take much longer and be a lot more difficult.

But it still felt like a slap in the face that Jassie had won with what Maeve thought was a mediocre entry, at best. Carob-chip cookies.

"But you enjoyed them, didn't you?" She laughed and patted Baker on the head.

She whined instead of licking Maeve's hand or barking. Or even wagging her tail.

"Baker?"

The dog had closed her eyes. She opened them now and

looked up at Maeve, whining again. Her body heaved, and she chomped on air.

"Baker? What's wrong, girl?"

She retched up half-digested cookies.

Panic gripped her heart. *She's sick.*

"What's the matter, Maeve? Your mutt giving you problems?" Jassie stopped next to the counter and folded her arms. "I told you to get her out of here, but you didn't listen."

"Shut up, Jassie."

"Whoa, somebody's twitchy."

Maeve ignored her and got up, walking a few steps from Baker. She bent and patted her knees. "Come on, girl. Come over here."

Baker struggled up, and as she did, she wet herself. And the floor around the counter.

"Oh, ew, what the heck? Your dog is—"

"Sick. She's sick." Maeve turned in a circle, desperate for help. There was a physician on site, the very same who'd sent the allergic judge to the hospital, but he wasn't a vet. And he didn't know Baker. "I've got to get her to Dr. Dale."

"If you leave now, you'll miss out on your prize," Jassie said, grinning. "Be my guest."

A judge had stepped onstage. He lifted the mic from its stand. "All right, everyone, we're just about ready to get started handing out the checks. If the first, second, and third place winners could come forth to the stage now, we'll get started."

Baker whined again, retching next to the counter.

Jassie flounced off, swaying her hips and pressing a triumphant smile at anyone who looked her way — which was just about everyone since she drew so much attention.

"There's our first place," said the judge. "Now, where's second and third?"

Maeve couldn't do this. If she stayed, she'd get her money,

but Baker would get worse. What if she died? This looked serious.

Go with your gut. That's what Mom would say.

"Contestant 987?" The judge's voice rang through the speakers and sweat gathered on the back of her neck.

Goodbye, bakery. Maeve couldn't risk Baker's life, even if it meant risking her dream.

She grabbed Baker's leash and led her down the aisle. The dog walked painfully slow, stopping to retch every now and again. This was bad. Maeve dropped the leash and bent over to pick her up. Thankfully, she wasn't too heavy. Baker shuddered against Maeve's chest.

"Hang on, Baker, I'm going to get you to Dr. Dale. Don't worry. You're going to be fine." She prayed it was true.

Tears welled, but she didn't let them escape as she ran for the exit.

"There she is." Jassie's voice through the speakers. "See there? She's leaving. She's disqualified. Ha!"

"Ma'am, give me the microphone, please," the judge said.

Maeve blocked out Jassie's laughter, the whispers and shouts following her as she ran from the tent and out into the parking lot. She made it to her car, put Baker down, then unlocked the door and helped her into the back seat. The poor dog vomited all over the floor. Maeve stroked her back.

"It's going to be okay." She got in and miraculously the engine started on the first try. She tore out of the parking lot as fast as the tires would carry her. "We're going to see Dr. Dale. He'll help you. It's going to be okay."

She had to keep telling herself that, or she would fall apart.

She couldn't lose Baker now that she finally had her back.

～

MAEVE PACED the length of the Pretty Paws lobby, grinding her teeth.

Dr. Dale had rushed Baker through the minute he'd seen her. He hadn't given Maeve any information at all, but his expression stayed with her. He'd gone wide-eyed, his lips drawing into a thin line.

What's wrong with her? How did this happen?

She was fine one moment, then sick the next. Maeve didn't understand. What could it have been?

She marched up to the receptionist desk and placed her palms on it. "Hi."

"Yes?" The receptionist, the redhaired young woman who had been here during the fight with the Rottweiler, glanced up at Maeve, then glanced back down at the computer screen and frowned. "No, nothing yet."

"I've been waiting over half an hour. I need to know what's going on with my dog. Can you please find out from Dr. Dale?"

"He's with Baker right now. He'll be out as soon as she's stable."

"But I have to know. You don't understand, Baker is … she's important to me. Please." Maeve pressed her hands to her stomach. The panic cramped her insides with fear.

The woman rose from her desk and rounded it, coming out and placing a hand on Maeve's shoulder.

"I understand," she said softly. "But you have to be patient. Dr. Dale is taking care of her. He's not going to let anything happen."

"You're sure?" Maybe questioning this woman was a bad thing to do — she did seem to know what she was saying, and she'd helped with the Rottweiler before, too — but Maeve couldn't help it. She needed to know.

"Take a seat. Let me fix you some green tea for your nerves."

"Yeah. Thanks." Maeve sat. The chairs were threadbare,

like they'd been clawed one too many times, or like a million other worried people had picked at them. She placed her hands in her lap and tugged on her fingers. "I just — she's been in there so long."

"He's not going to let anything bad happen," the redhead said again, and this time, it sounded like a promise. She disappeared briefly behind a door, then came back out with two steaming cups of tea. She handed one to Maeve and kept the other for herself, and they sipped together in silence.

Maeve waited for what felt like an agonizing eternity.

Then the door to the back opened, and Dr. Dale stepped out, hands tucked into the pockets of his white coat. He beckoned to Maeve, and she practically jumped from her chair in her hurry to reach him.

"What is it?" she asked, jerking to a stop. "Is she okay?"

"She's fine now. Or she will be. She's stabilized," Dr. Dale said. "Would you like to see her?"

"Yes, yes, please!"

He led her down a short hall and through another door, this time into a wide-open room lined with countertops around three walls and a stack of cages against the fourth. There was a pole holding fluids and lines running into one of the cages at the bottom. Dr. Dale nodded toward it, and Maeve dropped to her knees in front of the door.

Baker was there, half-curled at the back of the cage, breathing quietly and not looking up, but also not vomiting and whimpering, so that was probably progress. The line from the fluids was taped down tight on her front paw.

"What's going on?" Maeve whispered, not wanting to disturb Baker's rest. "What happened to her?"

"Chocolate poisoning," he said.

She blinked. "Chocolate? How?"

"Eating it, I would guess," he said, not unkindly. "You got her here fast enough that we don't need surgery, but she'll have to stay here overnight for fluids and observation."

"I don't get it. She didn't have any chocolate."

"Are you sure?"

"She came with Emma from the shelter, who said Baker hadn't eaten anything yet, then she hung out with me at the contest. I didn't feed her anything—"

The blood ran straight out of her head, leaving her dizzy.

How dare you accuse me of cheating? Jassie's words echoed through Maeve's head.

Guilty much, Jassie?

"What is it?" Dr. Dale asked, crouching down beside her and looking intently at her. He had very blue eyes that pierced, even through his thick round glasses.

"Carob-chip cookies." The words tumbled out of her as she thought them. "Jassie cheated. She said her cookies were carob chip, but she must've been lying. And I let poor Baker eat them, because I was mad at Jassie. I should have stopped her." Maeve buried her face into her hands. "I'm the worst dog owner ever."

"It's not your fault. You believed they were carob, not chocolate."

But if she hadn't been so petty about Jassie beating her, Baker would be fine right now.

And she'd have a ten-thousand-dollar check in her purse.

It served her right. Maeve would happily take this as karma, as long as Baker was okay.

She lowered my hands to peek up at Dr. Dale.

"Are you sure she's going to be all right?"

"As sure as I can ever be." Dr. Dale smiled. "You did right getting her in here fast enough. It's good to see Baker finally has an owner who cares about her."

Maeve opened her mouth to correct him — she wasn't technically her owner — but she planned to fix that.

Tonight.

Chapter Twenty-Eight

BAKER'S MOUTH tasted ashy and her eyes were scratchy, but none of that mattered. Maeve was here.

Her voice broke through the sleepy haze of sickness and drugs, then she was reaching out and opening the cage door and encouraging her forward to sprawl across her lap.

Baker went willingly, trying to ignore the annoyance of the needle in her leg and the line trying to tangle in her paws. She laid her chin on Maeve's thigh.

"There you are. You had me really scared."

She wagged her tail, although it took some effort. Earlier, she barely been able to move and she'd made a mess on the floor. Dr. Dale had lifted her with gentle hands and done things she didn't like, but now, she felt a lot better. Especially with Maeve here.

Maeve stroked the fur on her neck. "There you go, puppy. I'm here." Her blue eyes glimmered with tears.

Was she upset?

Baker lifted her head, and Maeve kissed her right between the ears. "This is my fault, Baker. I should never have let you go back to that shelter. I'm so sorry. If you hadn't gone back, you wouldn't have been so hungry and you wouldn't have eaten Jassie's cookies."

She poked at Maeve's chin with her nose, and Maeve laughed softly.

"I'm so glad you're all right," she said. "I can't believe this happened. Chocolate poisoning."

She licked her hand.

"Those cookies." Dr. Dale's voice cut through the quiet moment. Baker hadn't even noticed him crouching nearby, she'd been so fixed on Maeve. "They were meant to be carob?"

"That's what Jassie said. She had to list all the ingredients on her entry form, just like the rest of us." Maeve sighed, shaking her head. "Jassie actually cheated. She nearly killed Baker. It makes me so mad, I could just … ugh."

"Don't get mad, get even," Dr. Dale said. "You should report this to the folks who hosted the contest. If someone who can't eat chocolate tried one of Jassie's cookies, they might wind up getting sick, too."

"You're right," Maeve said sternly. "I'll speak to them about it. I won't let Jassie get away with something like this. She cheated, but worse, she hurt Baker. You know what? I'll go back tomorrow once Baker's well. I *can* fetch her tomorrow, right?"

"Bright and early." Dr. Dale patted her on the arm. "Go home and get some rest."

"Thank you. You have no idea how much I appreciate this." And then Maeve wrapped her arms around Baker again. She didn't flinch anymore, and the smell of fear had faded completely.

She stroked Baker's ears with her fingers and kissed her head again.

"I have to leave you here for the night. Dr. Dale will look after you, but I'll be back tomorrow to take you home. All right?"

Baker wagged her tail.

"I promise I'll be back."

Maeve promised.

None of the other humans she'd met kept their promises.

But she believed Maeve.

Baker was going home tomorrow.

She would eat shredded chicken and watch more movies and tolerate that annoying Macavity because it made Maeve happy.

And she would never, ever eat another cookie again.

Chapter Twenty-Nine

ARTHUR JACOBSON, the CEO of HealthNut, was the judge who'd fallen ill the day before. He'd agreed to meet Maeve at her favorite coffee shop — or at least it had been her favorite before she'd broken up with David and stopped going there to avoid running into him.

She'd gotten here early, enjoying the opportunity to sip some coffee while Baker sprawled near her feet, chewing on the toy she'd bought for the dog this morning, on the way to the vet.

"Maeve." Arthur Jacobson approached her table. He smiled and extended a tanned hand. "Glad to see you again. And sorry to hear you had to leave before the awards ceremony."

Maeve shook his hand, rising from her chair. "Thanks for coming to see me. I have something troubling to discuss with you."

He took a seat across from her, and the waitress ran over with a menu for him. "Just a coffee, thanks."

The waitress was gone again as soon as he'd said it.

"I hope it's nothing too serious. I'll let you in on a secret,

Maeve. I didn't have the best night. I spent it in the bathroom."

"I'm sorry to hear that."

He waved a hand. "The hazards of judging a baking contest."

"That's kind of what I asked you here to talk about." She took a breath. "Yesterday, you announced that the winner of the contest was Jassie St. Clair with her carob-chip cookies."

"They were delicious." He grinned.

"I'm positive they were. This is my dog, Baker."

"Hi, Baker." He waved at her, and she wagged her tail, once. She was still a bit timid, and Maeve didn't blame her for not being enthusiastic about meeting strangers. She wasn't about to go petting random dogs on the street, either.

"She ate some of the carob-chip cookies at the contest yesterday. And she got very ill."

Arthur frowned. "We had dogs growing up, and we often fed them carob treats."

Maeve retrieved a piece of paper from her tote bag — a report from Dr. Dale — and set it on the table for Arthur to read.

He glanced at it and his eyebrows went up. "Oh no."

"Jassie cheated by using dark chocolate instead of carob, and Baker almost died because of it," she explained, then held her breath.

Arthur was silent as he read. Finally, he withdrew his cellphone from his pocket and stood. "You'll have to excuse me for a moment, Maeve."

The waitress came back with his coffee, and Maeve ordered a refill. She needed as much caffeine as possible to get through this. What if he didn't believe her, thought she was trying to weasel her way into first place?

She didn't expect anything out of this; she'd already been disqualified for leaving early. She wasn't going to beg him for special treatment, she just wanted to see justice done for Baker. Cheating was cheating. Jassie didn't deserve to win.

Maeve bent and patted Baker on the head, then took a sip of her coffee.

Finally, Arthur came back to the table and took his seat. "Well, that settles it."

"Settles what?"

"I've spoken with the other judges as well as the board members." He cleared his throat and took a sip of his coffee that seemed to last forever. "Cheating is unacceptable and doesn't agree with our brand. Jassie's entry has been disqualified. And you, Maeve, have been chosen as our new contest winner. Congratulations."

She gasped.

Baker barked.

"Are you serious?"

"We'll do a new awards ceremony tomorrow and hand over your check. Jassie only won because two of the other judges were insistent on her cookies. I wasn't as convinced. Thought they were too simple." He grimaced. "Also, at the time I didn't realize she was the one who'd poisoned me. I'm allergic to chocolate."

"I can't thank you enough." Tears of joy sprang to her eyes. She rose from her chair. Baker barked again, and Maeve bent down and drew her into her arms. "We've done it, Baker. We're going to have our own bakery."

"That's what you're going to do with the prize money?" Arthur asked.

"It's always been my dream, but I haven't been able to scrape up enough to get started."

"Then it seems like we've chosen the right winner. This time around." He tapped his chin. "Maybe you and I should talk about additional opportunities. There's potential for a joint venture once you're all set up. You're officially a product line ambassador now."

Tears dripped down Maeve's cheeks. Baker licked one of them off. She laughed and hugged her tight.

She couldn't believe it.

Her own bakery.

No, not hers. *Theirs.*

Because what was the point of a dream come true without someone to share it with?

Epilogue

Two Years Later

BARKING Mad Bakery sat smack dab in the middle of the Logan's Creek shopping center, right next to Pretty Paws, in the space where that terrible pizzeria used to be. Needless to say, Maeve's complaints about the barking from the shelter were nonexistent. Taking this place had been the best idea she'd ever had, except maybe for her fresh concept: a bakery that served healthy treats to both humans and dogs.

That meant no chocolate was allowed on the premises, and owners could come in with their mutts and park their butts on the chairs or in playpens with their animals.

It had gotten easier and easier for her to be around dogs, thanks to Baker, and to the occasional bouts of play-fighting from Macavity, who had now taken to pouncing on the dog while she slept just to give them both a shock.

Maeve stood in the center of her bakery, hands on her hips and a grin parting her lips. The barking of happy dogs, the laughter of happy dog-lovers, and the smells of freshly-baked goodies hung in the air. And Baker stood beside her, leaning a little into her leg, lending her support, same as always.

This was exactly what I'd always wanted, even though I'd never imagined it quite like this.

"Maeve? It's almost time," Emma called from behind the counter. She'd started working at the bakery a few weeks ago, and was a total natural at handling the dogs and people who swept in and out. The customers liked her as much as Maeve did.

"Okay, coming!" Maeve hurried back behind the counter. "Where are they?"

"One sec." Emma finished ringing up a customer on our bronze cash register — vintage, from the antique store a few spaces down.

"All right, here." Emma bent and lifted the treats on their tray. "Doggy cupcakes. No sugar, no fat, no chocolate, extra bacon."

"Thanks." Maeve took the tray. "Look after the place for me while I'm gone?"

"Yeah, I'll try not to burn it down or anything." Emma stuck her tongue out at her.

She whistled to Baker as she hurried toward the bakery's open doors; the dog hopped up and followed her out. Maeve had enrolled them in Leslie's training course earlier this year, so they could learn how to communicate with each other.

Now, Baker barely needed a leash except when they were out walking together. Or when Maeve was nervous about it being too dark out, or about taking Baker near a busy street.

They took a sharp left and arrived directly in front of the Pretty Paws shelter's front door. Baker wasn't nervous about coming back here anymore. After six months of stopping by to drop off free treats for the pups, she'd come to understand that they were only visiting and that Maeve would never give her up.

Once she'd figured that out, she seemed to look forward to

it. She'd go from cage to cage as Maeve delivered treats to each resident, and she could swear Baker was comforting some of them.

By the time they were done, the ones who'd been the most frightened were calmer, and the ones who'd been the most excited were … also calmer. But in a happy way.

Baker nudged the door open with her nose, and they entered together.

Leslie stood behind the front desk, rifling through the mail, a frown creasing her forehead. But when she looked up, her expression transformed.

"Maeve," she said, grinning. "It's great to see you again. And Baker."

She came around the counter and bent low, extending a hand.

Baker put her paw in Leslie's palm for a shake — she was the only other human Baker seemed to bond with and trust.

"More treats?" Leslie asked.

"For the dogs." Maeve winked. "But I was hoping you'd stop by later on. I'm having a 'family' get-together."

That meant having Emma over for a movie night.

"That sounds great. If I can get all my work done before too late, I'll swing by."

Maeve set the treats down. "So, how have you been?"

"Oh good, good. Just the usual. Busy with the shelter. But I was wondering if you'd heard the news?"

"You'll have to tell me first. What is it?"

"Apparently, that, uh, ex of yours? David?"

"I'm familiar with him, yeah," she said, and pulled a face. In truth, Maeve didn't have any hard feelings about him anymore. He was just some guy who'd broken her heart. The love she'd found — with her friends, her customers, and most of all, with Baker — was so much stronger than anything she had ever had with him.

"Apparently, David has moved to Norway."

Um. "Okay."

"Yeah, Clara mentioned it the other day when she was in here. They were thinking about adopting, but she came in to let me know that David had left her. Some huge job opportunity. No idea what it was, and I didn't ask."

"Poor Clara." Maeve didn't exactly like David's model girlfriend, but she knew how it felt. David would do what he wanted — whatever he thought was best for himself. "But that's good news for me. I got sick of running into him around town."

"Didn't we all?" Leslie sighed. "The only reason I mention it is because, well, they didn't strike me as being the best animal owners. I was going to reject their application anyway. I have to do what's right for the—"

Three swift barks rang out, and a dog rushed out from the back passage of the shelter. A flash of what happened over two years ago — the black dog biting Baker, then her turning on Maeve — came back, and she put her arms out.

But this dog, a Dalmatian, didn't attack. It bounced into the room, ears flopping. It dropped low, sticking its spotted butt in the air, and wagged its tail at Baker.

Baker barked back and wagged her tail, albeit tentatively.

"Who's this?" Maeve asked.

"Charlie," Leslie said. "He's been ... an education in patience since he arrived. All he wants to do is run and play. Doesn't know when to stop."

Charlie barked and hopped in circles, then ran toward the counter where Maeve had set the treats. He jumped up, and Leslie barely managed to lift them out of range in time. "Eliza! Can you get up here and help out? Charlie's out again."

"We'll leave you to it," Maeve said.

Maeve whistled to Baker and went back to the bakery, making sure to close the Pretty Paws front door, just in case Charlie tried making a break for his freedom.

She patted Baker on her head before joining Emma behind the counter.

"You'll never guess who came in while you were gone."

"The pope? Queen Elizabeth? Margaret Thatcher?"

"Jassie St. Clair."

"She must've been lost." Jassie still lived in town, but after her embarrassing disqualification from the HealthNut competition, she'd kept mostly to herself. It had been a delightful two years — Maeve hadn't run into her once.

"She bought a treat. Can you believe it? And she asked to speak with you." Emma licked her lips. "I don't know, but I think she might want to apologize."

"Or lure me into some sort of elaborate trap."

Emma snorted. "Is it weird that I wouldn't put it past her?"

"She nearly killed Baker. If Jassie wants to apologize to someone, that's who she can apologize to."

"But what if she—"

"I don't really care. She belongs in the past, along with all the other things I just can't care about anymore."

Her future was way too bright to be worrying about Jassie St. Clair.

Maeve and Emma spent the day baking and serving treats. Baker played with some of the customers' dogs when she wasn't hanging around the register. As Maeve measured and mixed and kneaded, she sang a sweet song under her breath.

This was the life she was meant to live. This was the bakery she'd always wanted.

She only had it now thanks to one special dog.

At the end of a rewardingly-long day, she rounded the counter and drew Baker into a hug.

"Come on, girl," Maeve said, kissing her on the head. "It's time to go home."

When she needed a hand, she found a paw.

Struggling to finish her veterinary tech training and mourning the loss of her fiancée, Tessa wasn't exactly looking for a dog, but Princess found her anyway.

Get Reign of Terrier today!

A Note from the Author

Thank you for reading *Baker's Dozen*.

If you enjoyed this book, please consider writing a review of it on your favorite bookseller so other readers might enjoy it too. Just a couple of sentences. That would mean a lot to me.

Thank you!

Lori R. Taylor

Lori R. Taylor is the founder of TruDog, a lover of all animals, and author of the Soul Mutts series. It's her mission, vision, and passion to help humans understand the ways in which our canine friends make the world a better place. Lori's been helping to build businesses all her life, but her work at TruDog made her remember a dream she'd had forever.

She had always wanted to be a writer, and TruDog proved what Lori had always known. Not just that dogs made the world a better place, because of course they did, but that humans needed them more than they could ever possibly know.

In addition to her work with TruDog, Lori has helped to raise over 5 billion dollars for the Disabled American Veterans. She's not just an animal lover, Lori has a soft spot for unwanted or "broken" things and is their fiercest defender. Just ask Truman, the three-legged Great Dane that TruDog was named after.

As a little girl Lori dreamed of telling stories. She did that for brands for years. Now she's doing it like she's always wanted to, for you and with this series. Lori wrote Soul Mutts for you. Books to remind you of what you already know, but can't wait to feel again.